THE SHAMROGUES

First Challenge

THE SHAMROGUES

First Challenge

Niall Spratt

&

Patrick Meehan

ORPEN PRESS

Orpen Press
Lonsdale House
Avoca Ave
Blackrock
Co. Dublin
Ireland

e-mail: info@orpenpress.com
www.orpenpress.com

First published 1990, reprinted 1990, 1991.

Illustrations © Eamonn Elliot and Martin O'Grady

ISBN: 978-1-871305-57-9
ePub ISBN: 978-1-871305-71-5
Kindle ISBN: 978-1-871305-72-2

Printed in Ireland by Colorman Ltd.

For Niall Spratt

Contents

CHAPTER ONE

Druids' End, 435 AD

Warriors quaked as words of anger echoed from the Great Hall of Tara. The brave men stood outside two massive doors and heard King Laoghaire, who was a High King, issue a stern command.

"Now, Caffa, you must obey me. Do you understand?"

Caffa, most famous of wise druids in the land, knew better than to ignore the royal order.

"Yes, your Highness," he replied. "If you wish me to stop using my magic powers from this day onwards, then I will not refuse."

The old druid scanned the lofty hall and felt sadness touch his heart. He saw that the faces of those courtiers and lords who filled the gallery were also sad. Everyone knew that the druids of Ireland had come to the end of a glorious age. It had been filled with a boundless love for everything to do with nature.

Caffa bowed to King Laoghaire as best his feeble body could and shuffled through the studded doors

1

that had been thrown open. He left the fortress on the hill in a chariot drawn by a magnificent white horse and driven by Rottan, his protector and friend. They headed for the small settlement in the fertile valley of the River Boyne where his wife Aev awaited his return.

"What shall I do…What shall I do?" the old druid repeated to Rottan over and over again.

Once home, Caffa explained that he must give up his mystical powers. Aev shook her head in disbelief. They sat together in silence beside the crackling fire that blazed in the centre of the hard mud floor. The hut was made of upright pine logs and had a thatched roof of willow and straw with a hole at the highest point to let the smoke out.

"I have only this day left," Caffa finally said, "in which to practise my magic art. No longer will I be able to call on the Celestial Gods of the Sun and Moon to ask that our crops should grow strong and the mighty seas should flow and ebb in an orderly manner. No longer will I be able to foretell the future in order to avoid the many dangers that lie before us. And, sadly, no longer will I be able to speak with the wild animals of the air and land, or the fish that dart through our rivers like glistening silver. Indeed, we have come to a terrible day. The High King

2

commands these things because he feels that a time of change has been reached. I will obey."

The druid sighed and stared into the dancing flames. His favourite wolfhound Cu licked the back of his hand and a fat green-speckled frog croaked from behind a bronze shield that lay against the wall.

"Can you not do something before the sun slips behind the mountain and the day finally ends," Aev asked her downhearted husband. "Your great knowledge must not be wasted."

"But what can I do?" Caffa replied. He tugged at his long white beard and scratched his balding head.

Just then, there was a frightening sound as a rock beside the fire burst apart with the heat. Caffa and Aev flung themselves to the hard floor. This had happened before. A large fragment of rock whizzed through the air and lay smouldering on the grass outside.

"That is an omen," Aev said as she helped Caffa to his feet. "But what can it mean?"

The old druid dusted down his long grey habit and eyed the piece of stone that had escaped from the fire.

"Perhaps it wants my power," he joked and smiled a toothless grin at his wife. "It certainly flew through the air with the swiftness of an eagle."

"The stone looks more like a little soldier the way it stands so boldly on the ground," Aev whispered.

Caffa stroked his beard again. A certain glint, that Aev knew well, came into his eyes. An idea was forming in his mind. He stuck the tip of a grubby thumb into his mouth and then raised it into the smoky air above his head.

"I have it," he cackled. "I know what I must do before midnight arrives. Fetch four more stones the same size as that outside the door. Make sure they are all of different types of rock and bring them to the sacred altar. I will call a council of druids and explain my plans. We must move with urgency. Time hurries on."

Later, one hundred druids formed a circle in the open space between the settlement of huts and the dense dark forest.

"Caffa! Caffa!" they cried.

The old druid approached the altar on which Aev had placed the five stones. The altar itself had been carved from a huge flat boulder that had been left behind after the Ice Age, when a melting glacier had slid into the Irish Sea.

"My brothers and sisters of enchantment," Caffa yelled as loud as he could. "I have assembled you here to tell you of King Laoghaire's command to us all. The shadow of change is upon us. Before

4

midnight arrives, and after the sun has left the sky, we must forsake our ancient powers."

"Never! Never! Never!" screamed the druids in alarm.

Caffa, with Aev by his side, raised his bony arms and looked solemnly around him. A hush fell over the countryside as the old druid began to speak again.

"It is ordered and we must obey. Our duty is to serve the King and do as he bids."

"You speak the truth in this matter," the other druids said. "We will listen to your words though they trouble us greatly."

"Aev has gathered these five stones here for a purpose. We must band together and place our magical knowledge within them so that they can carry it to the future. Mankind may require our help some day. As our mortal bodies are not durable like these stones, we will entrust them with all we know."

Shouts of "Agreed! Agreed! Agreed!" rose to the cloudless sky. A single star twinkled in the great vastness above as a huge bonfire was set alight. Flames whooshed and sent thousands of tiny sparks skywards.

Caffa started the ceremony. He nodded to four harpists who began to play an eerie melody. Another druid, stripped to the waist, pounded on a goatskin drum. Others stamped their feet and hummed.

"All join hands," Caffa roared. "We must be united as one." He closed his eyes tightly and ran his hands over the stones.

The druids droned louder and the music of the harps and the beating of the drum got faster and faster. Caffa mumbled magic words of wisdom that only the highest of the high priests among the druids understood.

"Tamback negsu obar aercham, Manannan, Lu." He rubbed the tops of the stones with the palm of his hands.

The earth began to shake with the stamping of sandalled feet. A blustery wind raged down the valley and spiralled above the altar. It whipped at the hooded figures of the druids and whirled and spun as a luminous mist was drawn to its vortex.

There was a deafening thunderclap and a bolt of fiery lightning flashed down through the column of spinning mist. The five stones were thrown apart as the sudden blaze of flame from the skies struck the centre of the mighty altar. Sparks the colours of the rainbow showered on the frightened onlookers. They fell to the ground and covered their eyes. Caffa alone remained standing and chanted his words of magic louder than ever.

"Tambach negsu obar aercham, Manannan, Lu," he roared above the howl of the wind and boom of thunder.

As suddenly as it had begun, the terrible noise stopped. There was deathly silence. Caffa pushed the stones together with the tips of his spindly fingers.

"Oooh! aaah!" he cried, because the stones were scorching hot from the lightning bolt. But then his eyes opened wide at what he saw. The others still shielded their faces, afraid to look up.

Caffa grabbed the stones into the apron of his habit and sped into the dark forest. They squirmed and wriggled as he ran towards the mystical and enchanted mound that had been built as a passage grave three thousand years before, and whose entrance resembled the mouth of a narrow cave. He would secretly conceal the stones somewhere inside. No one else ever went there as it was a place full of playful spirits and unruly fairies. The mound would later be known as Newgrange.

The bright pale orb of the moon had risen to light Caffa's way. He entered the stony passage of the mound and laid the stones on the ground. The stones had taken on a new appearance. They had large eyes, round noses, and wide mouths that seemed to have a permanent grin. Their arms and feet were attached straight to their small bodies.

He spoke softly.

"Now my tiny friends. I must quickly instruct you in your varied tasks for the future. You have been endowed with the mighty power of the druids and must use it with wisdom and charity. A time that has yet to arrive will see many changes. You must be prepared to help when man has reached the stage when he threatens the very existence of our lovely planet."

The old druid shuddered at the thought. He looked at the five small creatures. They peered at him through the gloom of the passage, lit only by yellow moonlight.

"Now," Caffa said, "each one of you must have a name that explains your character."

He studied them closely in turn. "You," the druid said, and pointed. "Because you are the oldest type of stone here, you will be called Trom, the Wise One. You will be the leader. Next, Croga, the Brave, you will be champion and protect the others. Then we will have Sona, the Optimist... Glic, the Smart One...and last

9

but not least…Gorum, the Thinker, who must always consider the balance of each task you undertake."

Caffa seemed pleased with himself as the stone creatures whispered among themselves. Finally they looked at him, expressions of happiness on their faces.

"We like our names," Trom said in a deep voice. "But when can we start our work?"

"I'm afraid not for some time. It may be years before you get to use the magic you have been filled with. But do not worry. Your day will come."

"We look forward to it," they chimed together. "It will be a great adventure for us."

"Now for the sad part," Caffa said. "I must turn you back to stone and hide you until you are needed. You will be awakened and recalled when a spell which I shall engrave on the edges of a splinter of rock is read out. We must say goodbye for the present. I do not know if we can ever meet again."

"Goodbye!" they chorused.

A large owl swooped into the passage and landed on Caffa's shoulder. She hooted an urgent message into his ear and flew out into the night again.

"Midnight is almost upon us," Caffa said. "I must hurry. Farewell, little friends."

They blinked in the light of the moon and smiled.

"Maneg procto nate tercham, Manannan, Lu." The old druid waved a long finger over the creatures and they slowly changed back to stone.

Caffa took some sparkling magic dust from a small pouch he carried and sprinkled it over the stones. It would help them rest until they heard the spell that would give them life again.

With a small bone-handled knife, the druid loosened a floor slab and dug a small chamber in the damp clay underneath. He placed the five stones gently on the bottom. Having replaced the slab, he searched for a splinter of soft rock on which to engrave the spell. The owl hooted again. Time was running out. He quickly found what he was looking for.

Caffa went to the bank of the River Boyne. Its water rushed past him and reflected the light of the moon and the twinkling of the stars above. He carved deep notches along the edges of the rock in the form of a rhyme.

"Hurry! Hurry!" the river whispered. The old druid dug another hole in the earth and buried the rock. As he marked the spot with a tender oak sapling, the owl hooted twelve times. The Age of Magic was over.

Caffa felt tired and curled up on the river bank to sleep. His dreams were full of visions of the future. A future that needed to be treated with respect.

CHAPTER TWO

An Important Find

"I hope I'm not caught first again this time," Niamh, who was eight, thought.

She crouched down in the gouged-out hollow where the oak tree had torn itself away from the earth in the last great storm and heard her brother's voice carry through the stillness of the cold December evening.

"Here I come, ready or not. Keep your place or you'll be caught." Conor shouted, although he did not need to. He was eleven and always tried to sound like a grown-up.

"This is the best hiding place I've ever found," thought Niamh, as she peeped through the twisted roots.

To her right, the River Boyne, swollen with winter rain, flowed swiftly on its way to the Irish Sea. On her left and up on a rise she could make out the shape of a huge mound. It was Newgrange, a passage grave

13

built thousands of years ago. In the distance it looked strange and alone.

Niamh suddenly heard a noise coming from the rushes that grew on the river bank close by. She ducked back into the gloom of her hiding place and closed her eyes tightly. Her heart beat fast at the thought of being found before her older sister Sinéad.

The earth was damp and clammy where she knelt. Footsteps passed and moved away so that she could no longer hear them. Niamh knew that it had been Conor. Very soon, she heard her sister's name being called out.

"Caught you, Sinéad!" Conor said. "Come on quickly. We must find Niamh. It's going to get dark soon."

A little later, Niamh heard her sister and brother break into laughter. The sound of their merriment seemed far away. Perhaps they had given up their search for her. Or perhaps they could be playing a trick so that she would show herself. But she was not going to surrender as easily as that. Her hiding spot was too good to give away.

"Will they ever find me?" Niamh asked herself, when she had waited for what seemed like ages.

Twilight was settling in all around. She was becoming cold and a little frightened. Scraggly bits of wispy root, hanging like disused spiders' webs, brushed against her face. As the grey cloudy sky above became darker, Niamh wished for the game to be over.

"Hurry, Conor and Sinéad, hurry up and find me," she whispered to herself.

There was a scratching sound from beneath the decaying leaves in the hollow. Startled, she moved back, her shoulder knocking a clump of loose clay from some roots behind her. She screamed in fright as the muddy ball fell at her side. She looked down, not knowing what to expect.

The clump broke to pieces as it hit the ground and an oval shaped stone rolled onto the dried leaves.

The stone seemed to sparkle in the gloom for a brief moment. Niamh rubbed her eyes. Surprised, she picked it up slowly and began to examine it.

Having just heard her scream, the others called, "Come out, Niamh. We know where you are. The game is over!"

But Niamh was not in the mood to heed their call. There was something very strange about the stone she held in her hands. With fingers that tingled with cold – she had forgotten to wear her warm gloves – she brushed the remaining pieces of clay from the stone. It was almost the length of her school ruler and quite heavy. There were deep grooves engraved along its edges, but she could not see them very well in the darkening hollow.

"Come out, for goodness' sake," Conor shouted through the tight opening between the tree roots and ripped earth. "We must get home before it becomes too dark for us to find our way across the fields... Mam will be looking for us."

"That's right, lazy bones," Sinéad added in a bossy voice. "You probably fell asleep in there while we were searching for you."

Niamh sighed and began to crawl out, pushing the stone in front of her. It was always the same with older sisters. Especially when they were nine and a half years of age and Mam was well out of earshot.

When she emerged, Niamh saw that her brother and sister had already begun to make their way up the long slope from the river. They had not even bothered to ask why she had screamed.

"Wait for me," she called and picked up the flat oval stone. "I've found something good."

The tiny brown mouse who had been looking for food beneath the leaves in the hollow, peeped out and shivered. He saw Conor and Sinéad race their way back to Niamh.

"Give me a look first," Conor almost screamed when he reached his young sister. "I'm the oldest!"

Niamh tucked the stone under her jacket. At least she had made them come back for her.

Sinéad stood panting for breath with her hands firmly wedged into her pockets. Puffs of steaming breath escaped from her mouth and nostrils and she appeared to be angry. She was always trying to beat Conor at running, but never did.

"I won the game," Niamh said calmly. "You'd never have found me if I hadn't screamed. I could have stayed in there for ever and ever."

"Forget all that," Conor snapped. "Is it treasure?"

"Don't be so silly," Sinéad said. "How would anybody be able to hide treasure under the roots of that huge oak tree? It simply doesn't make sense!"

The brown mouse disappeared back into the hollow. He was not the type to listen to foolish human arguments. Anyway, it was becoming very dark and was certainly too cold to have your nose stuck out of doors.

"Here it is," Niamh said, as she produced the stone. "It glows in the dark and has funny markings down its edges. See!"

Conor whipped the stone from her hands and tried to look closely at it in the dark.

"You mean you called us all the way back down the hill for a rotten old stone?" Sinéad said, and started to walk away.

"This doesn't glow at all," Conor remarked, disappointment in his voice. "But there is something nice about the feel of it, and it certainly didn't grow these notches. We'll bring it home and ask Dad what the marks mean. Maybe they are a secret way of telling where treasure is hidden. Like a kind of code or something."

Conor tucked the stone under his right arm and held Niamh's hand as he led her away up the slope after Sinéad.

Trendorn, the badger, watched the three children head towards the brightly lit farmhouse where they lived. He knew them well and liked to see the games they played.

His own cubs had once played the same games along the river bank. Now, alas, they were all gone. Raising his head he sniffed the air. Through the night he would forage for something to eat. He was old and tired, and food was not as plentiful as it had once been. If only things could change, he thought, as he limped into a shallow ditch and made his way to the wooded copse on the far hill.

Once indoors, Niamh threw off her scarf and jacket and ran to her father, who had just come in from the milking shed for his tea. He went to the heavy white sink to wash his hands.

"I found an unusual stone, Daddy. It sparkled in the hollow where I was hiding." She turned and called to Conor who was still in the hallway putting his anorak on the coat stand. "Bring it in, bring it in. Daddy wants to see it."

Her father looked down at her and smiled. She was in the habit of showing him everything she found. Even when he had no time to spare, she insisted on getting his attention. She really was a character.

"Bring it straight into the living-room," her father called to Conor. "It's warmer in there, and your mother needs space in the kitchen to prepare tea."

Sinéad entered. "I'll help Mammy. I'm not really interested in silly stones."

Her mother flicked a lock of hair from Sinéad's forehead and handed her some plates to lay on the table.

The living-room was the biggest room in the house and always a happy, warm place to be. At the moment it was even nicer since Christmas was only eight days away and the room was full of colourful decorations that hung from the stout beams of the ceiling. The walls were covered with bunches of holly, ivy and painted acorns that had been gathered from around the farm. Beneath a wide mantelpiece laden with festive cards, a blazing fire crackled in the

grate. Niamh, Conor and their father sat before it on a big soft sofa.

"Now, let me see this wonderful thing you've found," their father said.

Niamh, who had taken the stone from Conor, handed it to her father. He rubbed its surface and studied it with great interest. The stone appeared to glow in the firelight.

"Look...Look, it's beginning to sparkle again," Niamh suddenly said, pointing with a shaky finger because she was so excited.

"That's only the reflection of the flames," Conor said gruffly. "Even I can see that!"

Their father raised his hand to quieten them.

"Stop bickering, the pair of you," he said sternly, and then grinned to show them that he was not really angry. "I'm afraid that I can't help you with any information about this stone. I have an idea that there may well be a story about the notches. Is there anyone you can ask about it? One of your teachers maybe?" Then he rose and went into the kitchen for his tea.

Sinéad came in as her father went to the kitchen.

"I heard what Dad said. I think we should see old Scribbles in school on Monday. If Mr Kane doesn't know what the strange marks are, then he shouldn't be a teacher."

"But this is only Saturday," Niamh complained. "We can't wait forever to find out."

Sinéad turned the television on and flopped into an armchair. Conor turned to Niamh.

"Monday will be soon enough. And Scribbles knows an awful lot about history, even though he seems to be out of it most of the time."

Niamh laughed out loud. Sinéad shushed her. Television was more important for the present.

"I just can't wait until Monday morning!" Niamh said. "I know that the stone is really something special."

Outside, from the edge of the wooded copse on the hill, Trendorn looked down at the farmhouse in the valley below. Everything was so calm and serene, the chimney letting a plume of smoke drift towards the sky. Three small dark bats flitted by and broke the spell. The night would be long and cold.

CHAPTER THREE

An Explanation

When Monday finally arrived, Niamh was up out of bed even before her mother had to call a second time. Since finding the stone, she had not let it out of her sight. She looked at where it lay on the floor. It made her think of something...a wonderful dream full of lovely visions that she had been having.

In her mind's eye, she saw a river, not unlike the Boyne, but with waters that sparkled in the sunlight and so clear that you could see the many fish that swam there. On the banks there were red deer who grazed on lush grass. High in the sky, an eagle soared in regal flight, the sun glinting about its wings. There was an old man with a wizened face who spoke gently to a large grey wolfhound by his side. The image was one of great peace and beauty. But it had only been a dream.

Outside, it was still dark. A fine sprinkling of white frost lay over the land and everywhere was perfectly quiet. Birds, tucked away in their favourite roosts, had not bothered to take to the sky in morning flight. Trendorn made his solitary way home, his feet cold and weary from the amount of walking he had done in his search for food. Grass, leaves and twigs, heavy with frozen dew, made muffled crunching sounds as he padded over them. High up in a stark chestnut tree, an old raven cawed loudly to tell all that a new day would soon begin. His name was Erc and he was nearly one hundred years old. Trendorn looked up at him and snarled in disgust. He was still hungry.

Niamh shivered and quickly put on her school uniform. She was the first down to the breakfast table and carried the stone with her. Porridge was her favourite on wintry mornings and her mother had given her a big bowlful.

When Sinéad and Conor finally arrived down, Niamh already had her hat, scarf and coat on. Although the stone made her schoolbag very heavy, she insisted on carrying it herself. It was tucked between her lunch and her schoolbooks. Finally, the three children were ready to go out into the cold countryside. They kissed their mother and called goodbye to their father, who was at the far end of the dairy yard. It was a fairly long walk to school and would take half an hour.

Scribbles, the history teacher, whose real name was Mr Kane, was a likeable sort of person. He had been given the nickname by pupils many years before. It came from his habit of jotting dates on the blackboard with such speed that only he himself could understand the scribbled figures. Niamh, Sinéad and Conor were lucky to catch him on his own before classes began.

Niamh explained where she had found the stone as she handed it into the teacher's eager fingers. His eyes lit up and he shoved his glasses back into place on his long, sharp nose. The children watched his changing expressions and smiled at each other. He turned the stone over and over again, mumbling quietly to himself. Then he laid it on an empty chair in the windy corridor where they all stood. He began to pace up and down. His head was bald except for tufts of grey hair that sprouted on either side. He scratched and tweaked at these until they resembled corkscrews standing on their ends. Niamh became impatient. She was about to ask the teacher if he could tell them anything at all about the stone, but the loud clanging of the school bell stopped her. Its sound echoed down the corridor as children rushed in every direction to their classrooms.

"Off with yourselves," the history teacher urged. "I believe this is a small type of Ogham stone. I'll explain more later, and I might even be able to tell you what the grooves mean. There is a message. Oh yes, indeed, there is definitely a message. See me during lunch break. Now, hmmmm...which way is it to my classroom?"

With that, he turned on his heel and sped off down the corridor.

The three children exchanged glances. Niamh was disappointed and looked glumly at the other two. Having to wait even a few more hours for an explanation was not easy.

"We'll meet here later," Conor said.

Time dragged by slowly, but then the bell clanged through the school again. The three children met where Mr Kane usually ate his lunch, in a remote corner of the library.

They found him with the Ogham stone in one hand and a thick jam sandwich in the other. He was perched on a high stool with a large open book balanced across his knees and his glasses resting on the tip of his nose as he read aloud. The children tiptoed to him.

"Ah, children," he blurted, munching a chunk of his sandwich as he continued to read. "Yes, yes. Very interesting indeed."

Mr Kane shifted on the stool. He tried to adjust his glasses with the back of his hand but a blob of blackcurrant jam from the half-eaten sandwich dropped onto the open page. There was a moment of panic when the book, followed by the teacher, tumbled to the tiled floor. Mr Kane rolled like an aged acrobat and rose to his feet, grinning at the children as though nothing had happened. He still grasped the Ogham stone and the bread.

Sinéad picked the book up from the floor. It was easy to find his place as jam made a very good marker. She prised the sticky pages apart. There was a drawing of the Ogham alphabet.

"You see," the history teacher said. "We will be able to make out what the grooves mean from this sketch. Now let me get a pen and paper and we'll have the message in no time at all."

Even Sinéad became interested now and she followed the others to the reading table where Mr Kane set down the Ogham stone, the book, and the remainder of his sandwich. The teacher went to work as the children watched closely.

"Ogham was an old Irish way of writing. Each groove is part of a letter or word. Already I have the beginning of a rhyming verse…'On the shortest day of winter, hidden by a magic spell. Lies the wisdom of the old ones, for how long now none can tell…'."

"Magic spell," Niamh beamed, tugging on Sinéad's sleeve with excitement. "I just knew there was something very special about it. And you'd called it 'a rotten stone'. And it was *me* who found it."

"Oh, stop being so childish," Sinéad said in a low serious voice. "I was only joking at the time."

"You really know your stuff, Mr Kane," Conor said.

The history teacher continued. He tweaked at a twirly corkscrew of hair with his free hand. With the other, he scribbled in his usual fashion as he wrote two more verses down. Then he read the final piece aloud. It only consisted of four words.

"Beneath the enchanted mound."

Conor was the first to speak, his voice almost shaking because his imagination was already running away with him. His face became flushed.

"We know where it means," he said "The mound is Newgrange. We were playing near there when Niamh discovered the stone under the roots of a tree."

"Yes, I suppose you're correct," Mr Kane agreed as he picked up the remainder of the sandwich and took a greedy bite. Only a corner of bread was left. This he threw towards the waste paper basket, but missed. The children looked at him as he wiped his mouth with the tips of his long fingers and then pushed his glasses back up his nose.

"What does it all mean? Tell us before we have to get back to our classes," Niamh pleaded. She could not help being a little bit cheeky. "Hurry."

"Yes, quite. Time is pressing," Mr Kane said. He leaned over the children and drew them closely together. They huddled in a small circle as though something secret was about to be told. The history teacher spoke in a whisper.

"This Ogham stone is obviously the work of some very wise druid who lived in Ireland long ago. He would have been a sort of priest in those glorious times...a Celt of the highest order, next only to the High King himself."

The teacher stretched to his full height and checked both left and right that they were still alone. He stooped and continued.

"According to the message, which is in rhyme form, the druids had to give up their powers. But before that was allowed to happen, they placed their magic knowledge into five small stones which were later buried in a secret chamber beneath the great mound. These rocks will come to life when a spell of enchantment is read aloud during the winter solstice. They will use their wisdom to tackle serious problems which affect both man and nature. At least that's what is engraved on the stone. But we know that it's only a fanciful tale; a myth invented by a people who loved everything to do with this planet."

"Oh, wouldn't it be wonderful if it was true?" Niamh said excitedly.

"When is the winter solstice?" Conor asked.

"On the twenty-first day of December," Mr Kane answered. "In fact, in two days' time. But there is something important that you must do."

"What's that?" The three children spoke as one.

''The Ogham stone will have to be given into a museum. You see, it would be regarded as an archaeological find. What do you say?''

The school bell began to ring again. Sinéad looked at Niamh and Conor. Their faces were filled with disappointment. Mr Kane saw it too.

"Don't be so downhearted," he said softly. "You will be getting your holidays tomorrow. That should have you all dancing with joy. After all, what's this old stone compared to Christmas?"

Niamh and Conor nodded. "Yes, we promise," they said.

"Me too," Sinéad said.

The three children left the teacher in the library. Conor carried the note with the magic rhyme. Niamh hid the Ogham stone up her jumper and put it into her schoolbag when she reached her classroom.

Her head spun with what she had heard. Magic, a spell of enchantment, five small stones that could be brought to life – it was all too much for her. She could not concentrate on anything her teacher said. She went through the afternoon's lessons as if she was living in a dream. At long last the bell clanged to let everyone know that school was over. There was a huge rush for the doors and she could hardly wait to join Conor and Sinéad.

Very soon they were far along the winding country road which brought them home. The sky was heavy with dark grey clouds and an icy wind cut through the bare hedgerows and whistled across the bleak fields.

"What will we do?" Niamh asked.

"Exactly what we promised, silly," Sinéad scolded.

Conor was not as agreeable. He shook his head and kicked at every stone which lay in his path, hands stuffed deeply into his pockets. He had his scarf pulled up over his nose and only his eyes were exposed to the cold air.

Erc, the old raven, flew overhead and saw the three solitary figures on the black road below. There was something in the way they walked that told him they were not happy.

Humans were such moody creatures. They had all of the very best things that existed in the world, and still they were not always as pleased as they should be. He cawed loudly and flapped his aching wings to gain a little more height. Another tedious night in the tall chestnut tree was all he could look forward to.

Niamh was not going to give in without an argument.

"It was me who found the stone. It should be up to me what happens to anything I find. Scribbles is batty and hasn't got a clue about things that are magic. I just know that the message on the stone is true. Why should I have to give it up? Nobody has to know if I decide to keep it!"

"It's the rules…the law, to be exact," Sinéad said. "Anyway, we'd know if you didn't hand it in. And Mr Kane would find out when he gets back from wherever he's gone for his holidays. So stop being so childish." Sinéad could be really grumpy when she wanted to be.

"What about the chemical plant on the river?" Conor asked from behind his scarf.

"What about it?" Sinéad snapped.

"It has the river polluted that's what!" Niamh said. There was a twinkle in her eye which always appeared when she had a bright idea.

"We can do nothing about that," Sinéad insisted. "The owner would only laugh at us if we complained. He's a very rich man and wouldn't be bothered by what we had to say."

"But don't you see?" Niamh said. "What if the message is true? We would be bonkers if we didn't at least give it a try."

"Niamh is right," Conor almost shouted. "We have nothing to lose if it doesn't work. Then we can give the Ogham stone to the museum. It can do no harm."

"Yes, and we'll have our holidays," Niamh said. "It won't even interfere with school."

"When did Scribbles say the whatchamaycallit is?" Sinéad asked.

"The solstice," Conor cut in. "It happens in two days' time on the twenty-first."

"We could get the stones to come to life and ask them to do something about the pollution in the river," Niamh said.

"I think that both of you have gone mad," Sinéad protested. "Magic creatures that can save the world my foot. I wish you two would grow up."

"Please," Niamh groaned. "Let's at least give it a try. Then I'll be happy to agree to whatever has to be done."

Sinéad stopped in the roadway and looked at her sister and brother. They were serious. What harm could it do? Whatever, she thought. Let them make fools of themselves. "Okay. But if either of you ever tell any of my friends about how stupid we've all been, then I will never speak to you again. Now, let's hurry home."

"Brilliant! We'll have a great adventure in two days' time." Niamh said. "And it's our very own secret."

CHAPTER FOUR

A Name for the Strange Stones

There was a hush over the land. The great crowd of people that had gathered in the field in front of Newgrange Monument spoke in whispers. There was no particular reason for this strange behaviour, except that they stood on one of the most ancient and famous sites in all the country. Everyone was dressed in their heaviest clothing because the morning was bitterly cold. Some stamped their feet to keep their circulation going; others swung their arms about to stop the icy chill from seeping into their bones.

The sky slowly paled so that the twinkling stars faded and hazy streaks of tangerine took their place. Niamh, Sinéad and Conor were among the many spectators who had come to witness the solstice. Even the main chamber deep within the massive mound was full of people. Many had cameras, and there was a television crew who filmed all the goings on. Everyone waited with breath held in anticipation of a clear sunrise. They all looked towards the east where the sun would soon peep over the distant horizon.

If the sky remained cloudless, the sun's rays would penetrate along the stone-walled passage, right into the main chamber. It could only happen on this one morning in the year. The shaft of light would signal a rebirth, as, from this day onwards, the long dark nights would become shorter and shorter.

Conor brought his sisters away to the side of the great monument. It would not do for them to chant the rhyming spell in front of everyone.

Trendorn, who was on his way home, was amused. He watched from his favourite spot in the small wooded copse. The sight of so many people usually meant that there would be scraps of food to be had later. He put off going to bed and settled down to wait.

Erc had the same idea and perched himself on the very top of the mound along with many other birds. He watched Conor, Sinéad and Niamh sneak around the side of the monument. What was going on?

The rim of the sun gradually appeared over the edge of the earth. Its brightness slowly rolled across the countryside, like a carpet being spread by invisible hands. Closer and closer, the rays crept to Newgrange.

Niamh held the Ogham stone aloft as Conor and Sinéad prepared to read the spell of enchantment. Mr Kane's writing was difficult to decipher. Thank goodness they had rehearsed it a few times.

"The sun is almost high enough for its rays to hit the mound," Conor said. "As soon as they do, we'll begin. But not too loud in case we're caught."

"All of this bother for nothing," Sinéad said. "I want to get home and into my nice warm bed. I feel absolutely foolish standing here in this freezing field."

"Stop moaning," Niamh demanded and shivered. "We have to try."

People began a countdown in front of Newgrange. "Four…Three…Two…One…"

Conor and Sinéad began the chant. Niamh held the Ogham stone as high as her arms could stretch.

On the shortest day of winter,
Hidden by a magic spell,
Lies the wisdom of the old ones,
For how long now, none can tell.

Now the spell can be broken,
Power used for the good of all,
If the words are spoken by the pure of heart,
The very stones will hear the call.

Old knowledge stored in stone,
Buried long in the past,
Awaken now in present time,
To be used for good at last....

There suddenly came a deafening sound of thunder from deep within the mound, as though it was about to erupt. At the same time, the crowd gathered at the front, applauded and cheered at the top of their voices. They were thrilled to have been there to see the sunlight poke a finger-like ray right into the heart of Newgrange. With all the noise they had created themselves, they had not heard the other sound of rumbling. The sound that had frightened the three children.

"What's happened?" Niamh asked, when they had all run for safety behind an enormous upright boulder. "I don't know," Conor answered, and added, "I only know that my heart nearly jumped out of my mouth."

"It really scared me as well," Sinéad admitted. "But there's still a noise coming from that tiny gap." She pointed at a gap between two of the great rocks that surrounded the mound.

"Where?" Conor asked.

"That little gap that looks like it has a rabbit hole behind it," Niamh said, pointing.

The three children stared at the spot, listening intently. It sounded as if something was scratching to get out.

"There must be a frightened rabbit in there," Sinéad said. "Let's help it!"

Before they could stir, Niamh said, "This Ogham stone is roasting hot. I can hardly hold it."

Conor took it from her but quickly dropped it onto the frosty ground.

"Hissss…" Steam rose from where it had landed.

"Leave the stupid thing. It has only caused us trouble," Sinéad said.

Conor and Niamh waited for the hissing stone to cool. Sinéad went to the gap and shoved her

arm down the hole. She touched something and suddenly felt two paws, or it could have been a pair of tiny hands, grab her finger. She yelled and ran back to her brother and sister. There was not a mark to be found on her hand, but she was almost in tears.

The three now peered from behind the standing stone, amazed by what was climbing from the gap.

"It's them...it's them," Niamh whispered. "Woweee."

"Keep perfectly still," Conor said. "I can only see one little creature. Scribbles told us there would be five. Maybe he got the message wrong. Now, shush."

They watched in wonder. It was almost impossible to believe that what they saw was real. The creature, which was about twelve centimetres high, actually had a face, short arms and two tiny feet. It rubbed its eyes in the sunlight, stretched and then yawned. Up and down it marched and looked all around, taking care never to venture far from the gap. It had red hair.

There were more sounds from within. The creature walked back to the gap and seemed to call inside. Someone, or something, answered. Then more scratching sounds escaped from deep inside the mound. The children were stunned into silence.

Tiny pink fingers grasped either side of the low gap. Another head emerged and a creature who was of a different shape and colour clambered to join the other. This continued until there were five of them standing in a row at the base of the great mound.

They appeared to be having a deep conversation in some language the children did not understand.

"They're lovely little things," Niamh whispered from behind her hand. "I'm going over to them."

"No way." Sinéad held her by the sleeve. "It could be dangerous. They might turn you into salt or something worse. Or even a funny creature like themselves."

"Sinéad is right," Conor agreed. "They look like right little rogues. I wouldn't trust them."

"Don't be so cruel. They couldn't be rogues," Niamh said. "If anything, they're the opposite...."

"I wonder what they're called?" said Conor.

"I think we should call them Shamrogues!" was Niamh's reply. "Let's meet them...."

CHAPTER FIVE

First Task

Niamh slowly approached the five tiny creatures, trying not to startle them. She didn't want to make them retreat into the mound again. Conor and Sinéad followed close behind.

The three children stepped quietly over the rough grass which was wet from melting frost. Everything appeared new and crisp in the morning sunshine, and the countryside was bright and beautiful.

Leaning against the base of the giant kerbstones surrounding the mound, the little creatures allowed the heat of the sun to warm them.

They had spent hundreds of years in the stuffy secret chamber where Caffa the druid had hidden them. It was a wonderful treat to be out in the fresh air once more. Their heavy eyelids were closed to shut out the glare of the sun as each one recalled endless years in their cold hiding place. That was until a dark shadow fell across them. Five pairs of eyes opened

all at once and the creatures cringed when they saw three huge children standing over them.

The creature who had emerged from the mound first stepped boldly to the front of the small group. But when Niamh knelt to have a closer look, the brave creature stumbled backwards and hid behind another, who was immediately pushed forward. This strange little creature was different than the others since as he had a beard. It was white, as were his bushy eyebrows. He stood his ground as the children ventured a bit nearer. The main trunk of his body was whitish-grey in colour. He raised a hand when he felt they had come close enough.

"Hibbly hopplepop harump," the creature said sternly.

"What did he say?" Niamh asked the other two. They knelt down beside her.

"He's talking in some foreign language," Conor replied.

"Shush," Sinéad said. "He's going to speak again!"

"Derut rer rumbok semdum?"

The being waved his tiny hands about and then turned a little to one side. He pointed to the rest of his group. They clung on to one another and their eyes opened wider than ever.

"We're your friends," Niamh said quietly, "Friends...friends. We won't harm you. We need your help."

Trendorn, who still sat where he had settled down earlier, watched the peculiar happenings. He was bewildered by it all and looked up at Erc perched in the tree above his head. The raven merely ruffled his black feathers and cawed twice. He, too, could not understand what was going on at the side of Newgrange.

"We won't be able to talk to them at all," Sinéad said. "How can we ask for help if they can't understand us?"

Conor, who had picked up the Ogham stone when it cooled, spoke sadly. "After all the trouble we went to. Now that we have brought them to life, they don't know what we're saying. I really wish they could speak our language."

The Ogham stone began to burn his hand again and he dropped it for a second time. It smouldered on the wet ground.

The bearded creature saw it fall. He rushed to the grooved stone and called to the other four. They didn't seem to care how close they came to the children. Something was suddenly more important to them.

"Caffa," the grey one said. "Ogham. Ogham!"

"They know what it is," Niamh cried.

"Ogham...Ogham," the five creatures chanted. The one with the beard put up his hands to quieten them.

"Trom," he said in a strong loud voice. "My name is Trom. When the boy wished on the Ogham stone, the remainder of its power was used up. Now we will be able to speak like you do. But, from our size, you can see that we were not born as humans are. We know that we were once stones, but what are we now?"

"You're Shamrogues, of course," Niamh said. "What else could you be? And you are all such colourful creatures!"

"I never got to make a wish," Sinéad moaned.

"Quiet," Conor said. "It would be polite to introduce ourselves. After all, it's what adults do when they meet other people."

The children told the Shamrogues their names and Niamh explained how she came across the stone. The Shamrogues were very interested in what the children had to say. Trom explained to Niamh, Sinéad and Conor how wise Caffa had put all the wisdom, knowledge and, most of all, the magic of the druids in them.

"Not only that," Trom continued. "Caffa gave us the real characteristics and personalities of human beings so that we might understand their feelings and their weaknesses. But now it is our turn to let you know our names. I will begin with myself."

The three children were really enjoying themselves, being beside ancient Newgrange in the shelter of the mound, and with the December sunshine all around them. It was more than they could ever have wished for. Much more than that, to be speaking to five creatures they had brought from the distant past was nothing short of wonderful.

Trom began. "You already know my name. I was chosen by Caffa to be leader of our small band and to act with wisdom in all matters. I have been endowed with great magical powers and will use them to the best of my ability. Each of us, as you can see, is a different colour. This comes from us being various types of stone. I myself was once quartzite which is a dull whitish rock. I must now ask the others to tell you a little about themselves."

"My name is Sona," a pink creature with brown hair said in a girl's voice. "I am always happy and Caffa said that I am an optimist. That means I always see the good in everything. It's great that you found the Ogham stone because I love being out here."

Sona cartwheeled in the grass and squealed in delight.

"My turn. It's my turn next." A creature, who was mostly green, tumbled three times and then performed a handstand. "Look at me. I'm so smart. My name is Glic and I'm the craftiest little creature in the whole world. I could walk on my hands forever. Watch me, watch me. Ouch!"

"Sounds like a boy to me," Conor said. "I'm better at handstands than he is. Look! He's fallen over already. Anyway, he looks like a piece of marble."

"He's a little nutter if you ask me," Niamh added.

"All boys are show-offs," Sinéad scoffed.

The yellow creature who had acted as scout and sentry came up to the children. "I'm Croga. It's my job to look after this lot. I have my hands full."

Niamh whispered to Conor and Sinéad, "Sounds like Granny Kelly speaking. I bet it's a she creature. Take a look at her wild red hair and the way she walks with her arms folded. I wouldn't like to step out of line with the likes of her around."

"You're perfectly correct, my dear," the last creature, who was blue, said. "They call me Gorum. I consider myself to be an expert on most subjects. So many fools rush into all kinds of trouble without bothering to consider the risks. Not me. I think things out first. For instance, I must say that the way you brought us to life was quite rash. Why, we could have been absolute monsters and might have eaten you up as soon as you approached us. But, oh no, you didn't think about that. And what's more…"

"That is enough, Gorum," Trom flared. "These lovely children have called on us for a reason. Let's ask them why."

"It's the pollution in the river that has us a bit worried," Sinéad said. "Can you help? So many people and animals depend on what you can do with your great gift of magic. We are helpless against powerful people with lots of money. They don't care about who or what they ruin to make even more money."

First Task

All eyes were on Sinéad. It was the first time that Conor and Niamh had heard her speak with such concern. They were very happy to have her on their side, as she usually disagreed with every idea they had. They smiled and patted her on the back.

"Well spoken," Trom said. "Of course we'll do our best to help in whatever way we can. Caffa intended that we would be of use to mankind and nature. This will be a chance to see if the powers he gave us will work after all these years. It can be our first task. A test to start us off."

"Hooray!" Sona cheered. "We have something to do at long last."

"Hold on. Who has caused all this pollution?" Gorum asked. "We can't go gallivanting across the countryside without knowing more of the facts."

"Agreed," Trom said. "We will need some details so that we can form a plan of action."

The children told the Shamrogues about the industrialist whose house was at the top of the valley. He lived in a plush mansion and his name was Bertram Savage. Already a multi-millionaire, Mr Savage wanted to be richer. The chemical plant would go on polluting the river until all life in the foul waters no longer survived.

"That is a terrible story," Croga said. "I know what I'd like to do with his sort."

Gorum said, "Nothing nasty, I hope. We are peace-loving creatures after all!" He scratched his head as though he was already working on a solution. His blue hair was a mess from all the brain scratching.

"Why do you all have such strange-looking hair?" Niamh asked. "And how are your bodies coloured so brightly?"

Gorum was about to answer, but it was Trom who actually did.

"You see, this growth is really a type of moss. Our bodies are so bright because, as we were changed from stones to creatures, there was a lot of heat involved. In fact, we nearly glowed. When we cooled down, we were these lovely colours. I would say that magic had a great deal to do with it as well. Honest to goodness pure magic. I think it is time for us to part for the present. We know what we must do. We will retire to our hidden chamber in the mound and make our plans. Tell no one of this meeting. Goodbye."

Trom got his small group together and they began to clamber back through the gap in the kerbstones. The children waved to them and Niamh blew Trom a kiss when he looked back for the last time before climbing out of view. Tiny echoes escaped from the hole as the Shamrogues made their way deep inside Newgrange.

The children had succeeded in what they had set out to do. Perhaps now things in the valley might change. They certainly hoped so. There was still one last thing to be done. The Ogham stone would have to be brought to a museum.

Trendorn and Erc had seen everything. However, because of the distance between them and the mound, they had not heard anything that was said. They were glad when the tiny creatures disappeared out of sight and the children wandered off home. Finding food was all they could think about.

Chapter Six

Problem Solved

"The plant must stay in production night and day for every hour of the year. And this includes Christmas. I need people who are not afraid of work!"

Bertram Savage hammered the shiny top of his desk with a stubby finger. His large body heaved in an over-sized office chair and his eyes rolled in a flushed round face. He glared at David Poddle, his unfortunate plant manager.

"If I've said it once, I've said it a thousand times. Find me people who work without complaining!"

"Yes indeed, Mr Savage," Poddle replied, wringing his bony hands. "It was only that they wanted Christmas Day off so that they could be with their families."

"Soppy twits," Savage said. "I'm leaving it up to you to see that there is a full shift of workers at all times. Understand?"

Poddle became pale. "Yes, Mr Savage, if that's what you want."

Savage grinned and looked around his flashy office. A beautiful Christmas tree stood in the corner. Nothing had been spared on buying the very best lights and the shiniest tinsel. The plant boss was pleased. Things were going according to plan and there was money to be made.

"Now, Poddle, since it's Friday evening, I'm taking my leave for the weekend. I'll phone at intervals. It's Christmas, I know. But see there's no slacking. Goodbye!"

"Right, Mr Savage. And…Merry Christmas!"

The boss swept out of the office building and made his way to a long black limousine which a chauffeur had waiting at the entrance for him.

David Poddle slumped into a small chair which stood in front of his employer's desk. With the big man gone, perhaps he could relax a little. He stared out the window.

Just then a black raven landed on the sheltered window sill and looked in at the sad expression on the man's face. It was Erc. His body hugged the corner of the sill and shivered. It was the coldest day of the year and snow could not be very far away. Life would become even harder then.

Poddle rested his heavy head in the palms of his hands. The thick double-glazed glass on the window protected him from the cold outside. "I wish that I could swop places with you," he said, although Erc could not hear him. "You really have it made. All you have to do is fly here, fly there, and rest when you feel like it. You have the freedom to go where you please, when you please. People leave out food for you and the fields are full of seeds and you're a very lucky chap indeed. If you had my job, having to deal with my boss, then you'd really have your work cut out."

Erc sat on the window ledge and trembled with the cold which bit into him.

"My, my," he thought. "That office looks nice and snug. Humans know how to live. They've even cut down a fine tree so that they can have the beauty of the forest inside in the warmth. The lights shine with the brightness of a city. I wish that I could swop places with that skinny man who could not possibly have any reason to be sad in such luxury. If he had to struggle hard for every single mouthful of food, he'd really have his work cut out."

It was Christmas Eve and a great quietness had descended across the countryside, although in homesteads everywhere there was the hustle and bustle of fevered activity. Last-minute shopping had to be done, clothes prepared and laid out, and children of all ages to be bathed. Finishing touches had to be put to many Christmas cakes and puddings, and then it would be off to bed for eager children who wanted the night to pass quickly. The following morning would see them up bright and early to find what great things Santa had left for them.

Inside Newgrange mound, it was very, very dark. This fact did not bother the Shamrogues at all. Their large eyes could make out the tiniest detail in the gloom.

"We will carry out our first task as soon as night begins to grip the land," Trom informed his companions. "We have had enough time to get used to our new bodies. I only hope that our magic works as well as when Caffa gave us the power."

"Weeee, Haaa!" Glic screamed with delight. He slapped Sona playfully on the back and began to dance. "Didder-e-a, Didder-e-o. Here we go!"

"Give it over," Gorum said. "This is no time for dancing. We need our wits about us. After all, we have to get to the industrialist's house first. We're Shamrogues, not tracker dogs. How are we supposed to find out where he lives exactly?"

"Oh," Sona exclaimed in a little girl voice. "That should be an easy one."

The Shamrogues looked at each other and then at Sona. Since the solstice, when they had come to life again, Sona had come up with lots of ideas and suggestions. One had been to change Newgrange into a grand palace. Another, to turn winter into summer. And yet another, to sweeten the rain so that it tasted of honey one day, and ice cold milk the next. Where her imagination came from they had no answer whatsoever. Now they listened with their minds full of doubt that she could possibly have anything sensible to say.

"We will simply ask directions, of course. There can be nothing easier than that. Can there?"

Croga folded her arms across her chest. She drew her body to its full height and gave a kind of snort. "Heh! And I suppose that I would be the one to have to carry out such nonsense. Imagine me having to say to some ginormous person: 'Can you tell me the way to Mr Bertram Savage's house? I must see him on a matter of great importance.' Well, you're not going to catch me doing anything as foolish as that. Absolutely no way!"

"I'll do it. Give me a chance to do something," Glic said. "I'll charm someone into telling me."

"This is not getting us anywhere," Trom announced.

"Sona's idea is not really a bad one," Gorum said. "It could actually work. We don't have to ask a person. The animals who live in this area are bound to know. With the magic we possess, we should have no problem talking to them. I'm sure they'd be glad to help."

"There," Sona said. "I knew it was a great suggestion."

Trom decided to agree. "All right then, we will do just that. Let's make our way out and be on our way. Off we go!"

The sound of tramping of tiny feet echoed down the long tunnel that led to the outside world. It was great to be finally on the move; great to have the chance to test their new bodies and skills.

Trendorn, who was only beginning his nocturnal trek in search of food, was startled when one of the Shamrogues climbed through the gap between two massive kerbstones around the mound. He snarled. He regarded any other creature, who was not a badger like himself, as an enemy. The fur about his neck and shoulders bristled and he stood ready to attack. More creatures slowly emerged. He recognised them from when he had seen them with Niamh, Sinéad and Conor on the winter solstice. He backed away as they approached him. He snarled another warning lest they should come too near.

"We mean you no harm," Trom said, remembering that Niamh had spoken similar words when they had met. It seemed to be the proper thing to say when meeting someone who was not sure of you.

Trendorn stopped retreating. The tiny grey creature with the white beard had used badger language. How could it be?

"My name is Trom. I'm the leader of the group. Can you give us directions?"

The old badger knew where Savage lived and told them so. He had never met any creatures like these.

They certainly were friendly. He explained the route they would have to take and then bid them farewell.

Trendorn turned away and made straight for a rubbish tip where he often found something to eat. He realised that helping the tiny creatures had made him feel good. It was a peculiar sensation, but he liked it.

The Shamrogues made slow progress. Their small feet were of little use with the distance they had to cover. As they crossed a wide, muddy ditch, Trom halted them with an upraised arm.

"This will never do. It will take us days and days at this rate. We will have to figure out a quicker way of moving when we have to go so far."

"I think this is great," Sona said happily. She trod in the mud with feet that resembled flat pebbles. "Goodoo!"

Gorum did not like the squelchy mess he stood in. "I think that, since we are supposed to have magic powers, we should try using them. If we concentrate very hard on the place we're heading to, then something interesting might happen. Let's hold hands so that we stay together."

"Super," Glic grinned. "Let's give magic a try."

The five shut their big round eyes.

A solitary rat, with black whiskers and a long hairless tail, came sniffing along the damp ditch. The

Shamrogues, who stood in a small circle, did not see or hear her approach. She thought that at least one of the group might make an easy meal. One powerful lunge and a tasty morsel could be swallowed.

The rat crept closer and prepared to pounce. Before she could, a funny type of multi-coloured mist appeared to fill the bottom of the ditch. It swirled and swirled like a whirlpool. Soon, the mist was whipped upwards in a spiral like a miniature whirlwind.

Courage deserted the rat and she dived for cover into a disused rabbit burrow. When the dazzling commotion died down and eventually stopped, the rat peeped warily out. There was not one single creature in sight. Maybe, she thought, the mud had sucked them down into its murky depths.

Or could it have been the stagnant water she had sipped earlier that was making her see things?

The Shamrogues gripped one another firmly by the hand. In fact, they clung on for dear life. It was as though they were being swung around at a great speed on some giant merry-go-round. Faster and faster they spun until everything became a whizzing blur. They felt they were falling through the sky wrapped in a rainbow coloured fog. Having landed on grass, they rolled and bumped along the ground. A low garden wall prevented them from going any further.

"We're here!" Sona exclaimed, sitting on the ground and rubbing her eyes. "That certainly beat having to walk." She stood up but fell over again because all the spinning had made her dizzy.

"I'd love to have a go at that again," Glic said, laughing.

"That's all very well, but we'll have to touch up on our landings in future. I never knew that frost could make soggy ground so hard," Gorum moaned.

"Quiet, all of you," Croga whispered. "I can hear the padding of soft paws somewhere close by. Who or what can they belong to?"

"There's no need for you to ask. They belong to a huge guard dog the size of old Caffa's wolfhound. And here he comes bounding over to greet us in a most unfriendly manner." Trom stood waiting as the dog charged towards them.

Croga asked, "How on earth will I be able to defend you all against such a ferocious monster?"

"Simple," Sona beamed. "We'll hypnotise him with our wonderful magic powers. Concentrate!"

The Shamrogues, each with a hand raised, faced the enormous snarling dog, his bared fangs a frightening sight for the bravest of hearts.

"Stad!" Trom snapped in a commanding voice.

The gigantic dog managed another springing leap before he seemed to be tugged to a standstill by some invisible force. A comical look of surprise appeared on his face.

"Aha," Glic chuckled. "That's put a sudden stop to the menace. He resembles a big hairy statue."

Trom went to the animal and stroked its coat. "We'll wake him up as soon as we are finished what we have to do here. Now, follow me quietly. Come on."

The house turned out to be a large one that covered a huge area. It was painted white, but because darkest night had filled the valley, it appeared grey in the blackness.

High above, in the dome of the wide sky, stars flickered and twinkled like very small pieces of glass. But dense puffy snow clouds were creeping their way over the horizon. It became colder than ever, and the Shamrogues trembled.

"How are we to get in?" Gorum asked. "Everything is either locked or barred. The house is almost as impregnable as the fortress of Tara. We'll have to use our magic again."

"Our magic will not work in this case," Trom said. "We can magic ourselves anywhere we want to go in the open. But we must devise a method to tackle this problem of getting through solid barriers."

Croga studied the building. "There's soft white smoke coming from one of those pots on the roof. It must come from a fire inside in one of the rooms. If the smoke can escape so easily, then we should be able to enter without too much bother." She folded her arms in her usual way and leaned backwards to look up.

"I can use my magic to get onto the roof. Then I will have a marvellous slide down the soot tunnel into the room below. Once inside, I'll open a window for the rest of you. Please let me be the one!" Glic pleaded.

"Agreed," Trom said. "That will be a real problem solved."

CHAPTER SEVEN

Mission Accomplished

Glic stood on the ridge of the sloping roof beside a chimney stack that had two tall brown chimney pots. Smoke drifted slowly from only one of them. He quickly decided that it would be wise to enter the bungalow through the safer of the two – the one where no hot fire burned in the grate below!

The remaining Shamrogues saw Glic peer cautiously into the smokeless pot and then climb onto its rim. He sat there for a brief second and got his breath. One moment he was giving them a little wave and putting a tiny finger over his mouth and the next he was gone.

There was the faint sound of a voice calling "Wheeeeee!" and then a gentle muffled thud. The Shamrogues held their breath and listened for any indication that Glic had been heard. They seemed to wait for ages without anything happening. Then a window just above them began to open. A small, scruffy black head peeped over the window ledge. Two big eyes smiled.

"Climb up the trellis," Glic whispered. "Everyone is fast asleep in their beds. Quickly, but be careful!"

Croga helped Trom, Gorum and Sona onto the bottom of the wooden lattice beneath the window. As it was winter, no plants grew there. Then she began the climb herself. Soon they all stood on the ledge and watched Glic shake the soot from his bright green hair. When he had finished, they used the curtains to climb down to the carpeted floor inside the room. They listened for a second time and heard nothing.

"This feels like woolly grass under my feet," Sona said as she stooped to rub the carpet with her fingertips.

The whole room fascinated her, as it did the others. They had never seen such luxurious surroundings anywhere before. This was all so new to them and they realised that there were many things in the modern world they would have to learn about. Trom broke into their thoughts. "We do not have the time to take all of this in now. Mankind has certainly moved forward a great deal as far as these things are concerned. But we have work to do. Let's move without making any noise to where Bertram Savage sleeps."

Mission Accomplished

"Our footsteps will never be heard anyway!" Gorum declared. "Savage has done us one favour at least."

They quietly crept out of the room and into a long wide corridor that ran the length of the house. Luckily, many of the doors that led off the passageway were slightly ajar. They checked each room in turn. Decorations and all the paraphernalia of Christmas were everywhere to be seen. But there was not a sign of life. There was only one remaining door they had not checked behind, at the very end of the corridor, and it was closed. They studied it for almost a minute.

"Even if we pile on top of each other's shoulders and manage to make a kind of ladder that the lightest can climb, we will never reach that handle," Gorum said in a dejected voice.

Trom smiled and put an arm around his companion's shoulders. "For someone who thinks so deeply about everything, you forget that we have magical powers." He winked one of his large eyes beneath a white bushy eyebrow.

The Shamrogues stood back and stared at the brass handle until it soon began to glow. A reddish mist formed around it, and a wispy transparent hand started to take shape. Suddenly it grasped the handle and firmly turned it. The five smiled at each other as the door quietly sprung open. Magic was a great thing to possess.

They were in a big square hallway, and directly before them lay a broad staircase. Croga walked boldly to the bottom of the first step. She interlocked her fingers and formed a sling with her hands. "Come on, I'll hoist each one of you to the next stair. It shouldn't take us too long to reach the top."

"Me first," Glic volunteered. "Then I can help to pull the rest of you up. It should be fun."

They all jumped with fright when the old grandfather clock, standing majestically in the hall, chimed three times. Ringing resounded around the house and then there was silence, save for the measured ticking of the big clock.

Finally, they stood slightly breathless on a narrow landing with four doors.

Using magic again, the Shamrogues opened the first door with the mysterious misty hand. It hovered eerily above them as they inspected a very unusual room. Although they did not know it at the time, they were in a white tiled bathroom full of man's new inventions. The hand moved to the next door and slowly pushed it inwards.

Sona skipped lightly inside. "There are two beds in here. A little boy is fast asleep in each one," she told the others. "What will we do?"

"Move to the next room, of course," Glic whispered. "They must be Bertram Savage's sons."

The weird floating hand tipped the surface of the next door with an extended finger, and Glic slipped through the crack into the cosy bedroom.

"Two more in there," he said excitedly. "Two girls softly snoring their little heads off. They made me feel sleepy just looking at them." He yawned and stretched his short arms.

"There's work to be done," Trom said. "This is the last room in the house. Savage must be in there." Trom pointed. "Hand! Do your stuff. Then begone!"

The Shamrogues scanned the master bedroom from the safety of the doorway. Bertram Savage lay on his back in a deep sleep, snoring loudly. His wife slept soundly beside him and murmured quietly into her pillow.

"Right!" Trom uttered in a hushed whisper. "Take up positions around the man – as closely as possible. Now we must tune our minds together."

The Shamrogues entered the room. Glic scampered up the flex of a bedside lamp. He leapt onto the padded blue headboard and smiled cheekily. Croga helped Trom onto the low bedside locker, while Sona and Gorum climbed the loose duvet cover and made their way to the head of the bed without disturbing the chemical plant owner or his wife. Croga remained on the floor and focused her full attention on the man's pale face. She had already done more than enough climbing for one night.

"Snrrrrrr, ngaaaaaaa, snrrrrrrr," Savage droned.

At a signal from Trom, the Shamrogues all began to focus their magic energies on the big man's mind.

Savage began to dream. A dream that seemed more real than life itself. A dream that allowed him to see the river with the chemical plant perched like a shadow of doom over its banks. In his mind's eye, he could see the exit of the large round pipe as it emptied chemical waste into the once-clear waters.

Upstream, he could see the abundant life in the river. Fish, who jumped for flies and chased one another happily in crystal clear water, would no longer exist once they passed a certain point. Any living creature would be threatened in the same way if they ventured to swim, or, even worse, to drink the polluted liquid that had become a deadly cocktail of poison.

Then he saw something else. Downstream of the plant, the waters were becoming agitated and frothy. They were being whipped and stirred by something huge and invisible, almost like the river was getting into a state of anger and unrestrained fury.

Strange shapes rose from the fetid mess, which had taken on the thickness and consistency of slurry. Like demons who were trying to escape, the shapes made feeble attempts to climb out of the sticky concoction, but all to no avail. No sooner had they risen and bubbled to the surface than they were sucked from view again. Then the horrible river with all of its foul pollution began to overflow its banks and swamp the countryside. Nothing could withstand the advancing rage of the life-destroying torrent. It rose up the valley and approached Savage's own home.

He watched as the scummy, seething threat swirled around the manicured gardens of his home and overwhelmed everything in sight. It lapped hungrily at the doors of his house and crept up to the window sills. Savage rolled and turned in his sleep, but the terrible dream would not go away.

All at once, the loathsome deluge smashed through the doors and windows with frightening force. It rushed into the rooms of the house and swept away anything that stood in its path. Christmas presents for friends and relations were driven against walls and then swallowed by the noxious matter. It hissed and splashed, and rose higher and even higher still. Decorations were torn from the walls, and the Christmas tree was seen for the last time as it disappeared into the ooze.

The polluted flood slowly made its way up the stairs in the hallway and started to seep into the children's bedrooms. Savage whimpered, but he was unable to stop the encroaching flow as it began to lift the beds. His four children slept for a while but were soon awakened by the whirling motion of the repugnant mess.

"Daddy, Daddy! Save us!" they screamed at the top of their voices. "Help! Help! The filthy water is trying to tip us out of our beds."

Their father struggled in his sleep. He waved his arms about in utter despair. "Don't touch the water. Hang on and don't let it get near you. Watch

the water....It's full of dangerous chemicals...
CHEMICALS!"

In his dream, he could see the children's beds being
slowly drawn to the top of the stairs. The deluge was
retreating and the staircase had become a torrential
waterfall. The beds were getting dangerously close.
If they reached the top step, the children would be
flung into the suffocating mess. They would be lost
to their father forever.

"Stop, stop! This can't happen to my lovely
children! Stop or I'll...I'll...HELP!"

"Oh, stop all your silly blatherin'," Savage's wife
shrieked as she shook him awake. He was sitting up
in bed and continued to wave his arms, his hands
clutching at empty air.

Bertram Savage ceased struggling and looked
at his trembling hands. He turned to his wife and
smiled sheepishly.

"It was all only a dream. Ha, ha. I was only
dreaming. Our children are safe...SAFE!"

"Hmmph," his wife said. "You and your
nightmares."

He watched her turn onto her side and punch her
pillow. In a moment, she was whistling in her sleep.
He let his gaze wander around the room. Everything
was peaceful. But the Shamrogues had seen it all
from their various hiding places.

Croga cautiously looked around the room. Glic, who had fallen to the floor when the plant owner suddenly sat upright, crept beneath the bed. Trom stood rigidly concealed behind the chunky base of a lamp, daring not to move for fear of discovery. Sona and Gorum had quickly dived behind the pillows on the big bed. Only their hair and large eyes could be seen peering above the frills of the pillow cases. Now they all watched the big man's actions.

Savage picked up a bone-shaped thing from a bedside table and put it to the side of his face. He then stabbed at several buttons on a flat square object that lay on the table. Then a strange thing occurred.

"Hello...Poddle? It's me...Bertram. I'm calling to tell you to send home all of the plant workers who are doing their shifts right now!"

"Sorry, Mister Savage...?" said the voice that came from the object in Savage's hand in a muffled whisper. "Send the employees home? Are they all sacked?" Poddle's voice was full of disbelief.

In the total silence of the bedroom, the Shamrogues could hear everything.

"Not at all, Poddle. It's time they went home. I want them to be there when morning arrives so that they can be with their children. Children are very important."

"What? Children? Have you been drinking, Mr Savage? Or is it....That's it! You're having a Christmas practical joke. Ha, ha, ha. Very good, sir."

"Give up this nonsense, Poddle. I have not been drinking, and I mean what I say. Send them home right now before any more of this night has passed. They will be paid as usual. Understand?"

"Yes, Mr Savage. They'll be very grateful for your kind gesture."

"Right, Poddle. Close the plant down and go home yourself. Great changes will have to be made come the New Year. Now, see to it!"

"But," Poddle was lost for words, "this doesn't sound like..."

"Do it!" Savage said. "And Poddle..."

"Yes, Mr Savage?"

"A very merry Christmas to you and your family. Goodnight for now!"

Bertram Savage replaced the phone on the receiver. He lay back and looked at the ceiling. "I feel better than I've felt in a long long time," he whispered. He closed his eyes and was quickly fast asleep with a contented grin lingering on his lips.

The Shamrogues quietly made their way from their hiding places and left the bedroom. Soon they were outside the house where a new surprise greeted them. Big fluffy flakes of snow were gently falling on the ground and they experienced real cold for the first time and shivered.

"What will we do now?" Gorum asked. "We'll freeze solid."

"Magic," Sona said, smiling. "Our magic will keep us warm. Now, think sunshine."

"It works," Glic said excitedly. "It really works. The thought of sunshine makes me feel warm all over!"

Trom raised his hand. "We must return to Newgrange. Morning will soon be upon us. Let us hold hands."

"Please," Sona said. "Could we not walk back? We're in no great hurry, and the snow is so lovely." She picked some up and it slowly melted in her hands.

"Yes," Glic added. "Everything is so bright and fresh. And we could throw snowballs."

"Why not let whoever wants to walk go together?" Croga suggested. "The rest can use magic to return."

"Not a bad idea," Gorum said.

Trom agreed. "We've accomplished our mission. Vote!"

A little later, Sona and Glic left Trom, Gorum and Croga. The three Shamrogues waved to their little companions as they set off on foot.

The magic spell was taken off the guard dog as a multi-coloured mist whisked the three away. The dog stood in confusion, wondering where all the snow had suddenly come from.

Outside the plant owner's house, Sona slipped and found that she could slide along on the crispy snow. It was a wonderful way to travel. Glic soon got the hang of it and picked up two small twigs so that he could ski on his pebble feet. They both raced over the snow as morning approached. They had to pass a small town with an old stone church at one end. They saw people going inside. Singing drifted up into the quiet valley. "Silent Night", the song began.

A thick blanket of the whitest snow covered the countryside as the pair reached Newgrange.

"Listen," said Sona. "I can hear bells above us."

They scanned the sky, but falling snow prevented them from seeing clearly. For one brief pause in the snowfall, they thought they caught a glimpse of a low shooting star as it streaked across the gathering brightness of the morning sky.

"Let's go inside to the others," Glic said. "It's time for us to rest until we're needed again. Ouch!"

A big snowball hit him on the back of the head. Sona laughed out loud with delight. "Come on." They climbed from view and into the mound.

Newgrange looked like a giant Christmas cake that had been specially iced for the occasion.

Further up the valley, Niamh awoke. She immediately noticed the extra brightness of the curtains in her bedroom.

"Snow!" she cried in wonderment. "It has snowed for this Christmas Day. Brilliant!"

Sinéad and Conor joined her at the window.

"Look," Sinéad said. Her breath steamed up the window pane and she quickly wiped it clean. "Look. There is no smoke coming from the chimneys of the chemical plant."

"And," interrupted Conor, "all of the big lights that are usually left on all the time are switched off."

"The Shamrogues," Niamh told them. "The Shamrogues have done as they promised." She jumped up and down with excitement. "What a lovely Christmas present. The most precious gift of all!"

"Speaking about presents," Sinéad remembered, "let's hurry downstairs and see what has been left around the Christmas tree for us. Whoopeee…!"

CHAPTER EIGHT

Day Trip

To be out and about in the glistening snow was a most mysterious feeling. Drifts and hollows of the cold powdery substance were everywhere to be seen. It was as though the colours of the whole world had been changed to a uniform whiteness. Even the sun appeared frozen and remote like a distant white ball. For Niamh, Sinéad and Conor, everything looked absolutely wonderful.

On the day after Christmas Day the children sat in the snug warmth of their parents' car and watched the countryside roll by and fall behind them. A trip to their granny's in Dublin was always a time for great excitement. She lived not very far from the city centre in a block of flats for senior citizens. She loved living in the busy heart of the metropolis.

Niamh, Sinéad and Conor rushed from the car when they arrived. They were slightly disappointed because there was very little snow about. But seeing Granny was much more important. She had been expecting them and stood waiting at her door to welcome them. There were lots of hugs and kisses before they finally went inside.

Then it was time to celebrate with a small party.

Afterwards, Conor and Niamh sat at the kitchen table and played board games. Sinéad decided to play with Granny's old dolls. It always fascinated her to think that her granny played with these old toys when she was a girl. They were dressed in hand-sewn clothes and smelled of times gone by. Sinéad gathered them into her arms and took up a favourite position of hers behind the couch. She lined up the dolls. Then she did something that children should never do: she listened to a conversation between her granny and her parents. But it was not as though she had planned to overhear what was said.

"Poor Ethel Crilly," her granny began. "They're trying to get her out of the place she was born in for goodness sake. What will happen to her now?"

Ethel Crilly was a spinster who lived alone in a big Georgian house nearby. From what Sinéad knew, the old lady had lived in the same house all her life.

Granny continued, "It really has me worried. Ethel has been my closest friend since we were young girls at school. Everything was alright while she had the landlord she knew so well. But when the kind old man passed away, his nasty good-for-nothing son

Day Trip

took over his affairs. The younger up-start is nothing but a greedy little penny pincher who thinks about nothing else except money."

"Shocking," Sinéad's mother said. "He should be locked up and the key thrown into the River Liffey!"

"Now, now," her father said in a low whisper. "As bad as the man sounds, he's probably perfectly within his rights. After all, the property is his. Isn't it?"

Granny had to agree. "But," she added, "it's only now that Ethel's alone and defenceless that Arnold Grimson wants her out. He sees a great opportunity to make lots of money by modernising the building and setting it out in luxury flats. And he doesn't care what he has to do to get his way."

"Shouldn't be allowed at all," Sinéad's father said and shook his head. "But what can anyone do? I'd love to speak to the landlord, but I doubt that it would serve any purpose if he's the type you describe. He'd probably just laugh at me. Grimson obviously feels that any agreement between his father and Miss Crilly was made to be broken. An ordinary person like me has no power to interfere." Sinéad heard her father sigh. "If only…"

"I've won! I've won!" Niamh roared with delight. "That was a great game. Let's play again. I'm very good at this. Come on, Sinéad, join us!"

Sinéad was glad of the opportunity to join her sister and brother. With her first throw of the dice, she leaned across the table and said beneath her breath, "We have to talk….Now!"

The other two looked questioningly at her. She pursed her lips and nodded towards the door.

Conor said aloud, "Phewww! It's very hot in here. Would it be alright if we went outside for a little while?"

"Okay," their mother answered, "off you go."

They gathered under an archway to shelter from the icy wind.

"What's all the fuss about?" Conor asked and blew into his hands.

"Yes," Niamh said grumpily. "It's freezing out here."

"Oh, be quiet," Sinéad snapped. "Poor Miss Crilly from down the street is having terrible trouble with her landlord."

Niamh and Conor's eyes opened wide. They were very fond of the old lady. What type of trouble could Miss Crilly be in? They got Sinéad to tell them all she knew and decided to check on Miss Crilly. The evening was getting dark. A busy stream of smoky cars, their lights switched on, passed them by as they walked towards Mrs Crilly's home.

Soon they reached the large house that stood on its own. Beside it was a derelict site with a tatty hoarding around its perimeter. Miss Crilly's house was in total darkness, the high windows black and gloomy.

Niamh said, "It's hard to believe that anyone lives here. Half the windows are broken, and the rest are so dirty that no one can see in or out of them."

"Let's knock," Conor suggested.

Sinéad disagreed and began to tug the other two along the street. "We can't disturb her at night. She might be frightened to answer the door in case it's her landlord, Grimson."

A shiver ran down Niamh's back as she looked over her shoulder at the looming house.

"We'll tell Dad that we would like to visit Miss Crilly before our school holidays are over," Sinéad said. "And the Shamrogues. They'll help us if we ask them. They're our friends and won't like what the nasty landlord is doing to Miss Crilly."

"That's a good idea," Conor said as he pulled up his collar against a sudden gust of wind that made scraps of paper and other loose bits of rubbish fly past them.

"Yes," Niamh said, grinning. "The Shamrogues are coming to Dublin."

CHAPTER NINE

The Enchanted Mound

Back at home, there had been a constant drizzle all through the night. The snow quickly melted as the fine rainfall turned it to slush.

Conor woke Niamh and Sinéad, who were having a well-earned lie-in.

"Come on, you pair, we have important stuff to do. Get dressed and hurry down to breakfast," he said.

Niamh, Sinéad and Conor made their way across the fields less than half an hour later. They passed along the banks of the River Boyne and saw the swiftness with which the water was making its way to the sea.

When they crested the brow of a small hill, the children saw Newgrange bathed in morning sunshine. There was a glorious reflected glare from the many stones that cover the mound, and a cold luminous mist lingered around its base. The whole area seemed deserted as they approached the ancient burial place of the great chieftains, and not even a whisper of wind disturbed the enchanted silence.

As they drew closer, their hearts began to beat a little faster. It was not every day that children got the chance to visit such an imposing monument, let alone with the purpose of calling on five magical creatures that no one else in the whole world knew existed. They peered into the gap between the two huge kerbstones, but there was little to be seen in the gloom.

"Yoohoo," Sinéad called into the small tunnel. The children listened for an answer, but they were disappointed. It was silent inside except for the echo of Sinéad's voice as it faded in the hollow depths of the interior.

"I'll give it a go," Conor said with determination. "If they don't hear me they'll never hear anything."

He took a deep breath. "HEYYYYY-AHHHHH!" he roared at the top of his voice. "ARE YOU COMING OUT?" But still there was only silence.

"We should have brought the stone," Niamh said.

Sinéad, distracted for a second, said almost dreamily, "The what?"

"The stone, stupid," Conor repeated and squinted as he tried to see deeper into the tunnel.

"Yes," Niamh asserted. "The Ogham stone."

Just then, there was a tremendous blast of noise from inside, causing Conor to fall back.

The entire mound seemed to rumble. The soggy ground beneath their feet appeared to shake and tremble. Conor remained sitting, listening to the strange sound. The children could hear one word being repeated over and over again. And it grew louder as the voices seemed to grow nearer.

"OGHAM – OGHAM – OGHAM – OGHAM – OGHAM – OGHAM."

Niamh and Sinéad retreated. The word Ogham had never been chanted with such gusto before.

Croga emerged first. She looked to left and right and then took a few steps forward. She looked at Conor who was still on the ground and then peered up at Niamh and Sinéad.

All the time, there was the continuous chant of "Ogham".

"Forward," Croga instructed. "It's the children!"

"Hooray!" Sona shouted, and leaped from the tunnel entrance.

The other Shamrogues quickly followed her. Trom took up the rear and stepped into the sunshine. After having tweaked the ends of his moustache and stroked his ample beard, he smiled at the children.

"You have summoned us again with the use of the magic word," the leader said.

"What magic word?" Conor asked, changing from sitting to kneeling on the soft earth.

"There is something," Gorum said, "that connects the past with the present, and it connects you with us...."

"Ogham!" Glic said impatiently. "All you have to say is OGHAM, and out we march to meet the three of you."

Gorum frowned at Glic. The little green creature was too smart and too cheeky by far. He was about to give the rascal a bit of his mind when Trom made his usual remark that meant he wanted silence.

"Harump," the leader said. "Let's listen to what the children have to tell us...and no interruptions from any of you."

Trom performed an awkward bow and made a sweeping gesture with one of his arms. It was as much as he could manage with his solid little body.

Niamh and Conor looked to Sinéad. Considering that it was she who had overheard the bad news about poor Miss Crilly, it was up to her to relate the story to the Shamrogues.

There was a lot of humming and hemming from the Shamrogues as she spoke. There were sighs and deep breaths, sad expressions, scratchings of the head, and pulling of faces. But each of the Shamrogues obeyed Trom's command by not saying anything until Sinéad had completely finished. She also explained about the state of the house and where it was before coming to a stop,

"This is a serious matter," Trom announced and let his eyes wander to the distant horizon where Sinéad had pointed during her tale of their trip to Dublin. In his wisdom, he knew that it must be a place full of danger. "We will have to go there," he said at last.

"Yippee!" Glic howled. "All we need are some chariots and a couple of fast chargers, and we can venture to the big house in the city."

"What's a charger?" Niamh asked. She innocently smiled when she saw the Shamrogues looking strangely at her. "Is it the thing that Daddy uses for the car?"

"Why, it's a horse of course," Sona said, laughing. "A big, fast, strong, brave horse. A chariot cannot move without one."

Conor saw that there was going to be a bit of confusion.

"I get it," he said to Niamh and Sinéad. "The Shamrogues come from so far back in the past that they don't understand a lot of things about today's world. There's no way that they could know about all the new inventions. Like cars."

Just then he spied something in the sky, high above where they stood. There was a long thin white plume being drawn across the deep blue heavens. At its tip, there was a tiny silver dot that reflected the sun's rays. They all followed his gaze and peered skywards. He stabbed a finger in the air.

"That thing way up there is an aeroplane. It's the size of a long house with metal wings, and it carries about a hundred people. They're heading for America."

There was the sound of tittering. Conor looked down. The Shamrogues shook with laughter. "I can see that we have a lot to learn," Gorum admitted when the laughter finally stopped. "Why don't we start now?"

"Oh no!" Sona and Glic chimed. "Not learning. We wanted to have some fun in the sunshine."

Trom looked sternly at the giddy pair. "Gorum is correct," he said. "Since we are now living in an age that is much different to the past, we should make an effort to pick up something about these new inventions. We would have thought that object was a fiery comet streaking across the sky."

Conor said, "We could start by going down to the roadside. It's as good a place as any to begin. At least you'll be able to see some modern types of transport. Cars mainly, similar to what our father drives."

"That's a great idea," Glic said. "It sounds as if some of this learning could be fun."

"Remember," Trom advised, "we Shamrogues must not be seen. We have the magic power to appear as ordinary stones when necessary. Should anyone come upon us, we cannot be detected. The children are the only people allowed to see us as we are. We can talk about some of the new wonders as we go along."

"There is something that has been troubling me," Gorum said, as they began to head towards the roadway. "That man, Bertram Savage, he spoke into a bone-shaped thing. We heard someone answer, yet we could see that they were not in the room. Was it magic?"

Conor was amused. "That was a telephone. They're used everywhere for people to talk to each other over short or long distances. They're very handy if you need to get in touch with somebody in a hurry."

"I thought as much," Gorum said and scratched his head.

"Would you like a lift?" Niamh asked. She stooped and laid her hands, palms upwards, on the dewy grass. Sona and Glic were fast to take her up on her offer.

Sinéad and Conor followed suit. Soon all of the little creatures were being carried along in the same way, Conor taking Trom and Gorum, and Sinéad conveying Croga.

"This is the way for us Shamrogues to travel," Sona declared happily.

It was not long before they came to a wide stone wall by the side of the road. Even the road needed to be explained as the Shamrogues had never before seen such a strange flat black surface. The children climbed onto the wall and let the creatures rest in their laps.

"There seems to be very little traffic today," Sinéad announced. "Everybody must be taking things easy."

Just then, a monstrous machine came around a bend in the road. It moved slowly and sputtered thick clouds of black smoke from a vertical chimney on its front.

"Here comes a tractor," Niamh said. "Daddy has one almost the same. They're used to do all types of work on the land."

The Shamrogues could be felt trembling on the children's knees as the tractor approached.

"It's a demon sent to gobble us up," Glic said.

"I think that we should retreat and regroup," Gorum insisted. "It makes good sense."

Croga swiftly climbed into one of Sinéad's pockets and peeped out with one eye open. She shook like a leaf as the huge tractor trundled closer.

Only Trom did not seem to be too disturbed. But he almost lost his nerve as the noisy machine drew level with them. The driver waved to the children as he passed, and then went around a bend further down the road.

"That was a close thing," Croga said as she emerged from her hiding place. "But I would not have let anything happen to any of you. Anyway, a tractor is a harmless smoky monster."

"That's right," Niamh said, chuckling. "Harmless!"

A sleek red car zipped along the road. It zoomed by in a flash before anyone could say or do anything. The noise was deafening for a brief moment, but soon faded. Just then a horse and cart came around the bend.

"Oh look, a chariot and charger," said Croga and everyone laughed.

The children knew the man, who sat easily in the cart with a heavy sack across his knees. He pulled on the reins and stopped when he reached them.

"Lovely day," he said and smiled. "I'm going towards Slane. Can I give you a lift?"

"No thanks, Mr O'Meara. We're just having a rest," Conor said.

"I see. And you've collected some very nice stones. That's a grand one you have there."

Without saying anything more Mr O'Meara leaned across and plucked Croga from Sinéad's lap. The children gasped. For the briefest second, Niamh saw a terrified eye as Mr O'Meara tossed the stone in the air and then caught it again.

"Very nice," he said. "Here, catch!"

Sinéad fumbled with Croga, but did not let her drop.

"Be seeing you. Bye!" Mr O'Meara said. "Giddy up, Nellie, we must be on our way... Hup!"

"Now, that really was too close," Croga said.

"Yes," Trom admitted. "I think we will call this lesson to an end. We've seen enough to be going on with. We'll return to Newgrange and finalise our plans."

The children carried the Shamrogues all the way back, and Croga was still shaking when they reached the gap in the kerbstones.

"We'll try not to let anything like that happen again," Trom insisted. "When can we get to Dublin?"

Glic said, "We'd love to see the big city as soon as possible. Even if it does have cars and the like."

"Yuk," Croga muttered. "And groping humans too!"

"Daddy is arranging with the National Museum for us to bring the Ogham stone to them. We'll be paying Miss Crilly a visit afterwards."

Sinéad explained that they would be going within the next few days. They would let the Shamrogues know exactly when.

"I can bring you in my rucksack," Niamh promised.

"Great," Sona exclaimed. "I can hardly wait."

"That's settled then," Trom said. "We will have time to prepare ourselves."

"Right," Sinéad announced. "Now we know the magic word, we should have no trouble calling you when it's time to go to Dublin."

"Ogham," Glic called as he disappeared down the tunnel, his shrill voice receding with him. The other Shamrogues began to follow.

"Goodbye till we meet again," Trom said, vanishing from sight.

CHAPTER TEN

Museum Visit

The visit to the National Museum was arranged. Earlier on the day of the visit, the three children hurried to Newgrange to alert the Shamrogues, but for the first time they experienced a problem in approaching the mound. A band of hardy tourists, not afraid to brave the cold, hovered about the monument taking photographs.

"Oh no!" Niamh moaned. "What can we do now?"

"There has to be a way," Conor answered. "Perhaps they'll go soon."

"But Dad said he was leaving in half an hour. And that was already more than ten minutes ago. We should nearly be heading back as it is." Sinéad looked anxiously at the great mound. A lone tourist stood almost directly beside the entrance to the Shamrogues' place of concealment. It was a woman with a large shoulder bag slung over one arm and carrying a camera.

"She's bound to discover the tunnel," Niamh said, her heart pounding as the woman began to run her hands over the surface of the kerbstones. She was stooping to investigate further when a man in garish yellow plaid trousers and a bright blue jacket called her.

"Isn't the texture of these rocks just wonderful, honey," the woman called back. "You can nearly feel the history of the ages running through your body when you touch them. Try it yourself."

"Aw shucks, I ain't in the humour to get my hands frozen off. Come on over here. The gang are gettin' ready to go."

The woman hesitated for what seemed like forever. Finally, after looking at the kerbstones once more, she joined the rest of the group.

"Honestly!" she drawled. "Those rocks have an aura that comes right off them. Like they were magic...or something. The whole place has!"

The group went into a huddle and spoke noisily among themselves.

"Are they ever going to go?" Niamh asked.

"They're settling into a heated discussion about Newgrange," Conor informed his sisters. "We'll have to attempt something else to call the Shamrogues. We can't go into the same field as those people. They're bound to become interested in what we're doing."

"That woman especially," Sinéad remarked.

"We can go to the next field on the right. It's very hilly and we mightn't be seen circling the fence at the side of the mound," Niamh suggested.

"Brilliant," Conor said in a low voice. "Let's go."

They quickly trudged through the long damp grass to the high fence and chose the spot closest to the narrow gap in the kerbstones. It was as near as they could get.

No sooner had they put their noses almost to the loose wire links of the fence than Niamh closed her eyes. If ever she wanted a wish to come true, it was definitely at this moment. The three children uttered the word together.

"OGHAM..."

It seemed to hang in the air as it carried across from where they stood. If this did not work, they could forget about smuggling the Shamrogues to Dublin.

But then a great thing happened. The sound of muffled rumbling came from deep inside the mound. The children watched excitedly as the sound grew a little louder, but they didn't experience any shaking of the ground, like before, as they waited for the Shamrogues.

The group of tourists stood back and stared with intense awe on their faces at what was happening. The woman with the shoulder bag and camera threw her arms around the man in the yellow plaid trousers.

"The mound is going to erupt like a volcano," she said. "If we don't get away from here, we'll be baked like crispy dumplings in roasting lava."

"No, no, honey!" the man exclaimed. "Why, that's only the sound of good ol' Irish thunder. There's no harm in it at all. Listen, it's almost stopped."

Croga, who had been leading the Shamrogues, blocked their exit when she heard the man's husky voice. Then she heard a woman speak.

"Sorry, honey, I don't know what has me so jumpy. It must be the thought of all the mystic power around here."

"I suppose you might be right," the man answered. "Let's get the show on the road. We've got a lot more places to see before the day is out."

The tourists went to the end of the field and left through the gate beside the narrow road. The children watched them leave in a white minibus. Then there was complete quietness.

Conor glanced at his watch. The half hour was nearly up.

"All clear," Niamh called to the Shamrogues. "Hurry and climb through the fence. We'll have to dash all the way home. Come and get into my rucksack!"

The Shamrogues ran from the tunnel towards the children.

"Quick," Niamh urged. "In the bag."

The Shamrogues jumped in. There were squeals and groans as Niamh, helped by Sinéad and Conor, hoisted the bag onto her shoulders. It was heavy, but she insisted on carrying it herself.

They were glad that Dad was not angry when they reached the car.

"You youngsters," he said. "How on earth do you always manage to get yourselves lost every time we're going somewhere special?"

"Oh, we weren't lost Daddy," Niamh blurted. "We were looking for…"

Sinéad nudged her with an elbow and glared crossly at her.

"The Ogham stone," their father said. "If that's what delayed you, then I have it here on the dashboard." He patted the notched stone.

"Great!" Conor exhaled.

"Right," their father said. "Finally we can get moving. No squabbling among the three of you on that back seat."

Their mother waved them off at the front door. They would be in Dublin and the National Museum in no time at all. Then on to Granny's and Miss Crilly's.

Niamh kept the rucksack on her knees and felt the Shamrogues pushing and wriggling inside the nylon bag. Travelling in such a confined space was a new experience and they jostled to reach the top so that they could peep out and watch the countryside from the car.

Conor saw a pair of eyes and two sets of tiny fingers push the flap of the rucksack to one side. It was Sona. She grinned, and without being invited jumped onto his shoulder.

He panicked and tried to grab the daring pink creature. His grip was too severe and Sona let out a piercing cry that made everyone jump.

She rolled from his shoulder onto his knees and then to the floor. He dived to pick her up.

"What's going on?" Dad asked. "I told you, no messing in the back seat. I'm having a hard enough time concentrating on the road. Kindly get yourself off the floor, Conor, and keep quiet for the rest of the journey!"

Sinéad helped Conor back onto the seat. He concealed Sona, who had quickly recovered from her fright, in his cupped hands. She gave him a smile as he returned her gently to Niamh's rucksack. There would be no more of that messing about in the car.

The children became excited as they turned into Kildare Street, where the museum stood.

After parking the car, they walked into the rotunda and main entrance of the big building. "Hello," their father said to the attendant at the reception desk. "My name is Michael Kelly. We have an appointment to see somebody about a stone that the children found near our farm."

The friendly attendant left them for a moment and returned with a young lady.

"Hi," she said. "I'm the resident archaeologist. I believe you've brought something for us to have a look at."

Their father introduced the children and they explained what Mr Kane their history teacher had told them. They also said that he had advised them to bring the stone to a museum, and that he had not believed the message on the Ogham stone to be true. He said that it was only a fanciful tale invented by a people who loved everything to do with this planet.

But, of course, the children now knew better. It was sad that they could not say so, and they didn't mention a word about their meeting with the Shamrogues, or how their new little friends were close by. The great secret was going to be theirs alone.

The young lady examined the stone closely. She rubbed its surface and then she took some notes. "This is very interesting," she said.

Meanwhile, the children examined the round mosaic floor with a pattern of the signs of the zodiac on its surface. They could see into the main hall, which was dimly lit and was full of glass cabinets with many historical artifacts on display.

Niamh whispered to the other two, "Wouldn't it be wonderful if our Ogham stone was to be put on show in there?"

"It certainly would," the archaeologist said. "But I'm afraid it might be some time before we can make a decision of that sort. Opinions other than my own have to be considered about what goes on view to the public. So, we'd be obliged if we could hold on to this for a while."

The children looked up at their father. "Well," he said awkwardly, "if that's the usual procedure, then I'm sure Niamh, Sinéad and Conor will agree."

"Mr Kane was right then?" Niamh asked. "The stone belongs here?"

"I'm not exactly sure yet," the woman replied. "In the strictest sense, this is not an Ogham stone as we know them. They are usually much larger and normally only carry the name of some great chieftain from the past. This stone is full of Ogham script, but it is more of an oracle or message carrier. Whoever wrote it used the old way of notches and grooves instead of letters. As far as I know, nothing like this has been found before."

The museum was definitely the safest place for something of this nature. After all, the children had no more use for the stone. Further, its powers had been expended, as far as they knew.

The children raced back to the car before their father. The Shamrogues had arrived at the conclusion that being out of the rucksack was better than remaining in it. The city was something they really wanted to see and being discovered did not seem to bother them. But they did look a little ashamed when they saw Conor wagging a finger at them through the window.

Sona and Glic, who had been happily swinging from the steering wheel, abruptly stopped. They bounced onto the driving seat and quickly scurried back to Niamh's bag. Gorum was standing on the top of a headrest studying the museum's grand exterior, while Trom and Croga were at the back window of the car watching everything going on in the street. They were all tucked safely inside the rucksack before the children's father returned.

"Two visits in the same week will be a surprise for Granny," Dad said. "Then you will have a chance to drop into Miss Crilly for a while. But not for long, mind you. We will have to be on our way before nightfall. I still have chores to attend to back home."

Granny was delighted to see them, but the children felt their fingers tingle with the need to get on with their task. As they reached the door, their father called after them, "Remember, we have to be leaving soon. Give Miss Crilly my regards."

The children paused for a long moment outside the old lady's house. Niamh felt the rucksack weigh heavily on her back, but was reluctant to ascend the four wide stone steps that led to the big door with the flaking paint. She hesitated as Conor and Sinéad climbed the steps and Conor used the brass door knocker that had not seen polish in ages.

"Bang…bang…bang," boomed through the house and seemed to be swallowed by its enormity.

"I doubt that there's anybody inside," Niamh said nervously. "We could always call back later."

The Shamrogues squirmed in the bag. "We've been brought here to help," Trom said. "Remember?"

Before she could change her mind, the hall door began to open.

"CREAKKK…" it groaned on unoiled hinges.

The children could see into the bare-floored hall. But as the door opened even wider, there was no sign of the person who stood behind it. They waited.

A friendly plump face with spectacles appeared in the dim light.

"Children," Miss Crilly said, beaming. "How nice of you to call. Come in."

Niamh ascended the steps and followed the other two. The big house smelled of freshly baked cakes and strong tea. The hallway was large and gloomy. A grey sleek-haired cat sat on the second step of the staircase. He flicked his tail and licked his lips with a long pink tongue. He stretched and walked slowly after the old lady's heels as she led the children to the back of the house. They entered a high-ceilinged room full of antique furniture and odds and ends. It was comfortable and warm. Orange flames danced in the big open fireplace, in front of which lay a red, threadbare Persian rug. The cat immediately took up his position on the rug, and, curling himself into a ball, began purring deeply. With his eyes closed, he appeared to be ignoring the children as they sat on the sturdy well-sprung sofa that had seen better days.

"I just knew that somebody was going to pay me a visit," Miss Crilly said. "How would you like some tea and scones? I won't be able to eat them all myself."

At the mention of food, the cat opened his eyes.

"That's typical of Percy," Miss Crilly said, noticing. "All cats become wide awake if they think there's a meal to be had. He enjoys nothing better than scones soaked in warm milk, then off he goes to sleep again."

The children laughed. Percy was smug about being the focus of attention, but then something caught his eye. The rucksack on Niamh's knees jiggled slightly. The cat sat bolt upright. This would require all of his attention. Something strange was going on. His ears pricked up at the peculiar sound.

"I'll only be a minute in the kitchen," Miss Crilly said. "Would one of you like to help me?"

Sinéad jumped to her feet and paused at the door. She pointed at the rucksack. Conor and Niamh understood. This would be the best chance they would have to allow the Shamrogues out of the bag.

"Wait!" Conor advised. The sound of footsteps grew fainter as Sinéad and Miss Crilly went into the kitchen.

"Now!"

Niamh opened the flap on the rucksack and peered inside. The five Shamrogues stared up at her.

"There's a rip in the back of this sofa," Conor said to her. "Hide our friends inside until they find somewhere better."

Percy's whiskers twitched as he sensed the presence of the Shamrogues. But he would be unable to do anything until the children left. He watched Niamh as she tenderly handled the tiny creatures and put them into the back of the sofa.

His tail flicked over and back, as though he had no control over its movements. His eyes narrowed and he imagined what it would be like to sink his sharp teeth into the coloured creatures.

The Shamrogues climbed in among the spiral springs and made their way to the roomy base. For Sona and Glic, it was great fun. For Trom, Croga and Gorum, it was more like work, but after some difficult manoeuvres, they succeeded in getting there.

Percy sidled up to the sofa and began to sniff suspiciously. A spring suddenly pranged and he jumped away in fright. From here on in, he would keep a close eye on things.

"Be careful," was all that Niamh could utter to the Shamrogues before Sinéad and Miss Crilly returned. They each carried a tray and laid them on a low table that Conor put on the rug in front of the fire. A smashing feast of hot scones and jam was quickly devoured by the three children. All too soon it was time for them to leave.

Miss Crilly noticed Percy's strange behaviour as the cat continuously circled the sofa and sniffed at it every now and then.

"My, my, whatever can be the matter, Percy?" she said. "I'm very surprised that you haven't touched the food I've prepared for you. If only you could speak!"

Chapter Eleven

Funny Goings-On

The Shamrogues rested in the base of the sofa and waited for a suitable opportunity to find a better hiding place. They could hear everything that was being said, and knew they would have only a short time in which to help the old lady. Glic climbed back up to the opening and cautiously peeped into the room.

Ethel Crilly sat in a bulky armchair beside the fire and wept silently. Percy, who was concerned about his owner's situation, detected an alert eye behind the rip in the torn fabric of the sofa. Without warning, he bounded over to the gap and slashed with needle-like claws at Glic. Luckily, the stuffing and loose bits of thread prevented Percy from wounding the little green Shamrogue.

"MEEOWWW!" the cat screeched in anger and frustration.

At the same moment, Glic screamed in terror and fell through the network of steel springs. "EEOWWW!"

The two cries blended as one and Miss Crilly thought only Percy was making all the fuss.

The cat struggled to get his claws free, but the more he tried, the more entangled he became.

"MEEOOWWW!"

Miss Crilly got up from the armchair.

"What on earth is the matter with you at all?" she said as she untangled him.

Percy lay on the sofa with his chest heaving from all the exertion, listening to what was being whispered below in the base. Miss Crilly could hear nothing. Her hearing had not been the best for many years. She had never told anyone of this problem. It was nobody's business but her own.

Evening quickly became night and Miss Crilly spent the lonely hours doing embroidery. The fire died down until it was nothing more than a heap of cinders and ash. Then it was time for bed.

"Come on, Percy," she called tenderly. "It's time for us to get some sleep. Tomorrow's another day. We'll have to take it as it comes."

"Sleep," Percy thought. "I've done nothing else but sleep all day long. And those creatures are bound to

be on the move soon. I'll sneak back down as soon as she nods off."

The cat stood and lazily stretched his sleek body, tearing his claws gradually over the surface of the rug. He would keep them sharp and ready for later.

The old lady's bedroom was on the first floor, but there was still another one above it. At the top of the house there was an attic full of bric-a-brac from the past. They lay there in the darkness, memories of happier occasions when Ethel Crilly's family occupied all the floors and the building resounded with laughter. Sometimes the old lady would imagine that she could hear her family around her still. She would suddenly look around expecting to see a smiling face, but no one would be there. Loneliness was a condition that took a lot of getting used to.

"Here, Percy," she said, patting the purple eiderdown beside her on the bed.

In no time at all, the old lady was sleeping soundly. But her hand rested on Percy's back. Each movement he made, she murmured softly in her sleep. He had no choice but to stay there.

Downstairs, the Shamrogues crept from their hiding place. The house was quiet and still.

The others followed Trom to a panelled door under the main staircase and climbed down the stone steps to the flagstone floor of the cellar.

Gorum examined an old disused mangle that had been used in the past to wring the water from washed clothes. It fascinated him and he tried to work out how it had once operated. He concentrated so much that the stiff handle jerkily began to turn all by itself. His magic was working on its own!

The others watched with growing excitement. If Gorum could perform and use his powers by merely thinking, then they all could.

Sona stared at the bulb in the centre of the ceiling. She jumped up and down with growing enthusiasm as it blinked as often as she wanted it to.

Glic wondered what the antiquated pushmower might be. He did not have long to ponder. As he watched, five rusty blades began to rotate and the machine moved towards him. Glic fled in terror, the grinding mower in hot pursuit, and jumped onto an overturned coal-scuttle with a jagged hole in its metal side.

Trom observed all. Each Shamrogue could function either alone or with the others. It was a useful discovery that would come in handy in the future. Just to be fully sure, he tried some magic himself. There was a piece of hosepipe hanging from a nail on one of the walls. Without knowing exactly what it was, or what it was used for, he thought aloud, "Move! Move, earthworm on the wall."

The hose began to wriggle and fell off the nail. Once on the floor, it started to writhe and coil. Somehow, the peculiar tubing performed as though it had been given life. Trom blinked his eyes and all movement ceased. The Shamrogues did indeed possess the magic powers that Caffa, the high druid, had intended them to have.

Upstairs, Percy the cat heard the racket from below, but Miss Crilly continued to hold him beneath her hand.

Meanwhile, in the basement, Trom walked to Glic's hiding place and peered in through the hole of the coal-scuttle.

"It's not safe out there," Glic explained. "That war machine with the five swords wanted to conquer me!"

"Well, it has given up the chase," Trom assured him. "However, you seem to have found a nice spot from where we can direct our operations. Make room for the rest of us."

"Those lovely smells of hot baked scones made my tummy feel funny earlier. I wonder could it be hunger?" Gorum said.

"Well, it's too late to worry about such things now," said Trom. "Climb in, everyone. Tomorrow is a big day."

CHAPTER TWELVE

Bottom Line...

Friday began as a bright, airy day, unusual for the second last one of the year. No sooner had Miss Crilly stirred awake than Percy was off down the stairs, three steps at a time.

The cellar was a place he was well acquainted with. He often spent many enjoyable hours stalking prey down there.

He abruptly stopped at the door beneath the staircase, expecting to hear the sound of gentle breathing.

But the Shamrogues had already heard his urgent descent on the wooden stairs to the hallway.

Percy moved without making even the slightest noise. Step by step, he crept down with the litheness of an animal well trained in the art of hunting. When he reached the flagstones, he hesitated and sniffed the cold air. Something made his whiskers tingle, and along his spine the grey fur bristled. His eyes scanned the cellar and a sixth sense brought his gaze to the coal-scuttle as he tiptoed across the floor.

"BOOM! BOOM! BOOM!" The house seemed to rock. "BOOMPITY, BOOM, BOOM," the heavy door knocker repeated.

Every centimetre of fur on Percy's body stiffened. Fear gripped him. The importance of his search vanished with the pounding on the hall door, for he knew who was knocking so aggressively.

Miss Crilly went nervously to the door and unlocked the wooden barrier between her and the outside world. Sunshine spilled into the hall. When the door was fully open, Miss Crilly stood back. The tall, dark, thin silhouette of Mr Grimson was framed in the light. He stepped inside and turned. Another shape of a stouter person bustled in after him.

"This is Charlie Mullarkey," Arnold Grimson said. "I've brought him to tend to a few things around the house."

"Hello, Missus," Mullarkey grunted. "I've brought my toolbox with me. This place looks as though it could do with the clatter of a hammer or the twist of a screwdriver here and there." He rapped on a wall with his meaty knuckles. "I'll start in the basement, shall I?" The man scratched a stubbly cheek, adjusted his well-worn cap, and pushed past Grimson and Miss Crilly. His heavy work boots

struck the floorboards with sharp snappy blows that repeated like pistol shots through the entire house. He disappeared under the stairs after a bout of wheezing stalled him.

"Sound bloke," the landlord said. "This cold weather doesn't suit him. Bothers his chest. But then, we all have our little problems. And now, are you ready to vacate this house by Monday?"

Miss Crilly handed Grimson her rent and he greedily counted the notes. He raised his eyebrows and stared down at the old lady.

"Well?" he enquired. "Lost our tongue, have we?"

"I don't know what to say," Miss Crilly answered, her timid voice quavering. "There wasn't enough time for me to arrange anything."

The landlord touched the tip of his pointed nose. "Ah, Miss Crilly. I'm terribly afraid that time is in short supply, my dear. Monday is the day for which notice was given to you, and Monday is the day I'm sticking to. My plans are made. It's too late to expect me to change them now."

"But Mr Grimson, where will I go?" Miss Crilly implored, on the verge of tears.

"Oh, I'm sure the authorities will give you a place. There's a nice old folks complex down the street. Try for somewhere in there, can't you? Now, I must go and see my man and tell him what to do."

Grimson left the old lady. She sat down on the stairs beside Percy. "All is lost, puss," she said.

The Shamrogues heard the landlord join Charlie Mullarkey in the basement.

"She'll still need some persuasion other than my words. Have you any suggestions?" Grimson whispered.

"Lots," Mullarkey said as he took a burglar's jemmy bar from the toolbox. "A loose board on the stairs would do the trick. She'll go head over heels to get out of this dump. Heh, heh, heh!"

"Don't be so stupid, you moron," Grimson said. "I want no violence. Just make things uncomfortable for the old biddy. I'm counting on you, and there's a nice little bonus in it if you succeed."

"I suppose the roof might be a good target to start on," the Shamrogues heard Mullarkey say as he and the landlord left the basement.

The Shamrogues listened to the footfalls on the floor above. Then the front door rattled on its hinges as it banged shut.

Glic climbed the steps to the basement door, which was open a crack, and listened.

"I'm just going onto the roof, Missus Crilly," the landlord's handyman said. "I have a nice long ladder outside. There's probably slates that need attention."

"It's Miss Crilly," the old lady asserted.

"Right Missus." He guffawed and went outside.

Glic signalled to the others when he saw Percy being picked up by the old lady and carried into the sitting-room. Miss Crilly closed the door.

"This requires some thought," Gorum said. "There's not much sense in all of us going to the roof.

We need to split up. We can work more effectively that way."

Trom considered the idea for a while. He stroked his beard and put on his wise face. "Gorum has it right again."

"Yay!" Sona exclaimed. "Where do I get to go?"

Trom looked at each of them in turn. "Croga and myself will remain down here in the basement. We're not very good at climbing or sliding. Gorum can keep us informed on what's happening on the ground floor. Sona and Glic can make their way upstairs. They will be able to travel through the ducting system that carries all the strange metal bars behind the walls and beneath the floors to the different rooms. I took a little wander last night while you were all asleep. It was a worthwhile task. Now, each of you to your places!"

What Trom was not aware of was that "the strange metal bars" were actually the pipes of the plumbing and gas system.

After a lot of tight squeezes the two Shamrogues reached the attic. They were just in time. They heard Mullarkey's footsteps outside on the roof. Then there was a crunching sound as the nasty man ripped a slate off the wooden slats that held it in place.

The brightness of sunlight invaded the grimy attic space. Tiny particles of dust fell and blew about like a shower of glistening atoms that caught the rays of the December sun. Mullarkey wheezed throatily as he was heard scampering over the apex of the roof.

"Now's our chance," Glic said. "Let's go out there and see what else he gets up to."

"Right," Sona declared. "Let's have some fun."

Mullarkey was about to throw the slate into the garden below, but before he lobbed it into the air a thought struck him. He saw a trickle of smoke rise from one of the tall chimney pots near him and he chuckled.

"Aheh!" he said. "Maybe I can smoke her out. This slate will make a perfect lid for that chimney. Nothing could work better than a blocked flue. Heh, heh, heh."

It fitted over the wide pot perfectly. He thought that a smoke-filled room below and a hole in the roof might be enough to drive the old lady out.

Carrying the slate, Mullarkey began to carefully edge his way up to the top of the ladder. But something very, very weird was happening.

Sona and Glic, hiding in a leaded gully, began to work some magic.

The slate slowly drifted out of his hands and up into the air. It remained there while Mullarkey rubbed his watery eyes and doubted what he was seeing. Then it zoomed in front of his nose and hovered as he struck out at it, clinging on to the ladder rails for his life. The tile made one and then two swooping passes at him, before suddenly slotting itself back into its place on the roof.

"It must be the medicine I took for my chest," Mullarkey thought in panic. "The instructions on the bottle say that a person shouldn't go up any heights after they've had a spoonful of the horrible stuff. And I...I took half the bottle." He gulped and began to feel extremely dizzy.

He shook so hard that the ladder began to tremble beneath his feet. Mullarkey fumbled his way down and lay on the grass in the back garden.

"Blasted medicine," he breathed. "Makes people hallucinate. No more of that stuff for me."

Miss Crilly looked out the back window and saw the handyman lying on the overgrown lawn.

"Lazy lump of blubber," she told Percy, but all the cat could think about was the little creatures the children had brought. If only Miss Crilly would open the door to the sitting-room.

"Meeow, meeow," he pleaded. Miss Crilly was bound to know what he meant.

"You're a terribly insistent pussy-cat," Miss Crilly said as she let him out.

Gorum called a warning to Trom and Croga, "That terrible cat is on the loose. The three of us had better hide."

Percy charged to the door under the stairs and ran headlong down into the basement. Graceful, stealthy creeping was of no importance to him now. He wanted the creatures so badly, he no longer cared about finesse.

As the cat was about to pounce on the coal-scuttle, Trom haughtily stepped out.

"I dislike doing this, but…Harump!" he raised his hand.

Percy stopped in full flight. He saw sparks in front of his eyes and was aware that he could not move.

"We're not your enemies," Trom said in cat language. "The children left us here to help Miss Crilly. I'll release you from the spell if you promise to listen to me without attacking. Wiggle the tip of your tail if you agree."

Percy, who had never experienced being put under a spell before, wiggled his tail for all he was worth.

Trom called Croga and Gorum to join them, and the leader explained who and what they were to the cat.

Mullarkey interrupted them. He tramped into the basement as they quickly hid under some old chairs that were strewn in a corner. The man went straight to the electric fuse board.

"The lack of electricity will do the trick," he muttered. "I'll just unscrew these. Now, let me see."

He began to twiddle with the fuses, slowly unscrewing them one by one. But no sooner had he left one and gone to another, than the fuses screwed themselves back. He tried again and again, but each time the result was the very same. The fuses refused to stay unscrewed!

Mullarkey removed them altogether and flung them to the floor, but they mysteriously rose again and hovered momentarily in front of his face, before screwing themselves back into the board. The man's face wore a bamboozled expression. It was all becoming too much.

Percy became so excited by what he was witnessing that he knocked over a chair which rolled out into the middle of the floor.

"Aha!" Mullarkey roared. "So, there's somebody hiding there! Well, I'll soon sort you out. You won't make an eejit out of me!"

He grabbed a worn sweeping brush and began to probe beneath the pile of chairs, but he felt nothing.

"The flashlight," he snapped, and went to his toolbox. He returned with a big rubber torch in one hand and a broom in the other. Still he could see nothing that might have toppled the chair. The head of the brush finally caught on something and he tugged and tugged.

Croga, Trom and Gorum pulled on the head of the brush with all their strength. Mullarkey pulled back, dropping the torch. Suddenly the head of the brush slipped from the handle and he tumbled backwards onto the ground. He roared in fright as Percy jumped on him and then shot up the steps.

Mullarkey had had enough, and fled from the house shouting, "No more blasted medicine for me in future!"

He ran all the way to Grimson's place of business and the landlord scowled when he saw the confused man.

"You thick!" Grimson said, when Mullarkey tried to explain what had happened. "Next you'll be telling me that the place is haunted. Get back to that house immediately."

Mullarkey refused. "I'm a sick man, Mr Grimson. I need rest."

"Well, you can have all you want for now on." Grimson said. "You're fired. I'll deal with this myself."

The cruel landlord decided to wait until the following evening, which happened to be New Year's Eve, before going back to Miss Crilly's. In the meantime, the Shamrogues got to know Percy very well.

Next evening, Grimson went to the big old house and let himself in with his pass key. He was careful not to let the old lady know. She sat in the sitting-room and continued her embroidery, as he removed his shoes in the hallway and crept upstairs. When he reached the attic, he lit a candle.

His arrival, however, had not gone unnoticed. Sona and Glic made their way up after him.

"I'll remove some slates from the inside. Mullarkey would never have thought of that!" Grimson said as he began to poke at the old roof with a moth-eaten umbrella.

"PHOOO!" sounded behind his back and the candle blew out.

Grimson relit it and returned to his task.

"PHOOO!" The candle went out again. Sona was having some of the fun she liked so much.

Grimson lit a match and it flickered for a brief second.

Then Glic made up his mind to have a go. "PHOOO!"

Grimson was not going to give up so easily. He struck another match. In the wavering light, a rickety rocking chair began to rock to and fro. The hairs on the back of his neck prickled at the sight. Then the match burned his fingers.

"Damn," he squealed and decided to change tactics, so he descended to the floor above where Miss Crilly sat. There was a hole in the creaky floorboards that he knew about and he went to it.

He put his hands around his mouth and got as close to the hole as he could. "WOOOOO! Wooo!" he wailed through the hole.

Grimson tapped on the wall and the floor, and then found a battered dustpan and a cracked glass tumbler in a dark corner. He rattled them off one another and the two items made a dull tinkling sound.

"WOOOO! Woooo!" he wailed. "BOOOOoooo! Waaaa!" Grimson jumped up and down on the bare floor.

Rattle! Tinkle! Rattle! Rattle! He hit the dustpan with the glass and jumped like a frenzied tap-dancer so that his pointed shoes struck the floorboards sharply.

Had Arnold Grimson known about Miss Crilly's problem with her hearing, he would have saved himself a lot of trouble and hardship. The landlord went on with his antics until he was near exhaustion. He sat on the side of a spring bed with no mattress and listened. The old lady was obviously not bothered with his pranks. He decided to wait for night.

Sona and Glic stood on the landing outside the door.

"Now it's his turn," Glic said as the house became dark. "OGHAM, ogham, ogham, ogham," the pair began to mutter behind their hands. They said the word deep and low.

Grimson sat up straight. Were his ears playing tricks on him? Or was somebody saying...

"Grab him! Hold him! Get him! Grip him!"

He became increasingly scared as the terrible voice chanted the threatening words over and over again. It was not the wind murmuring through the broken panes, nor the banging of the old pipes in the walls, nor the sound of creaking floorboards or skirtings. And he knew nothing about Shamrogues!

"GRAB HIM! HOLD HIM! GET HIM! GRIP HIM!" The chanting became louder and closer, the very walls pulsating with it.

The landlord put his hands over his ears but it didn't help. The words were hammering inside his head. When he could stand the pressure no longer, he dashed downstairs. As he ran through the hallway, he saw a slit of welcoming light pouring under the door of the sitting-room. Grimson gritted his teeth and passed by, but then paused.

"That fool Mullarkey was supposed to plunge this place into darkness," he thought.

Grimson had not allowed Mullarkey time to tell of his experiences in the cellar at the fuseboard. He would have done well to listen to everything the man had wanted to say.

Once down the stone steps of the basement, Grimson struck another match. "Nothing will blow it out this time," he said and put a protective hand up to shield it from any sudden draughts. He saw the rubber torch where the handyman had previously dropped it. The Shamrogues watched as he approached. The match went out with a sputter and the landlord tried to feel his way with his feet in the blackness. Soon his toe touched something.

Grimson bent to pick up the flashlight. He jumped back as something furry rubbed off the back of his hand and licked his sensitive skin.

"UGHhhh!" he uttered and fled up the steps.

Percy rejoined Trom, Croga and Gorum and gave a huge cat's grin. They wondered what would happen next.

Up in the hallway, Grimson rushed to get to the old lady in the room. In his haste, he came upon Sona and Glic who had descended from the landing above. Surprised, they stood stock still and appeared as two stones. He saw them with the help of the street light filtering through the fanlight over the front door.

A devious glint came into his eyes. He didn't know what two small stones were doing in the hallway, but he would use them to throw at whatever horrible creature had touched his hand.

"No, I'm not going mad," he said beneath his breath. "I'm doing the right thing. I'm brave...I'm brave. Nothing is going to frighten me any more!"

Grimson picked up the two Shamrogue stones and returned to the cellar.

Trom and Croga had moved the torch in his absence, after Gorum had come up with another plan. It was placed to one side of the basement near the back wall. They watched as the landlord crept down the steps.

Croga moved quietly to take her position. Her red-wild hair brushed off a filmy cobweb and a very tiny spider clung to the top of her head where it began to spin another web.

Grimson gingerly tiptoed across the flagstone floor. He edged to its centre.

There was a sudden glare of beaming light as Gorum thumped the button on the torch and the shape of Croga who stood in front of the lens of the torch, was projected onto the front wall. The landlord could not see anything for a second as his eyes adjusted to the startling brightness. When he could, the monstrous shadow on the wall grew bigger and bigger as Croga moved slowly away from the torch with her arms raised. And the movement of the spider's legs became visible as protruding tentacles from the monster's head.

Percy let out a howling scream. The man dropped his hands by his sides in utter confusion as Sona and Glic began to wriggle in his palms. He let go of them and they rolled away. Grimson retreated and stumbled upstairs.

The landlord burst into the sitting-room, almost in a faint. Miss Crilly put down her embroidery. He

began to mumble, but his head spun so badly that he needed to lie down. The old lady led him to the sofa.

"Why," she said softly, "you look like you've seen a ghost, Mr Grimson."

"Monsters, stones that come to life, threats of 'get him', confusion, rocking chairs, mysterious winds that blow matches and candles out..." Grimson wailed, shivering.

"I'll get you some nice tea and we can talk."

As the old lady was about to leave the room, Percy strolled in and sat licking his lips on the rug and purring noisily.

"No!" Grimson said, alarmed. "Don't leave me here alone."

Miss Crilly stopped and looked seriously at the gaunt man who motioned for her to stay.

"I want you to keep the house. It's not a lucky place. I don't want it. It's yours...yours!"

The old lady smiled. "I never thought I would hear those wonderful words. And just as the hands on the clock have reached twelve o'clock. Happy New Year, Mr Grimson. You have made me the happiest person in the world."

Grimson grinned sourly. "My pleasure, Miss Crilly. Yourself and your family have already paid for this house more than ten times over."

Percy rose and went to tell the Shamrogues. Although he suspected that they would be aware of Mr Grimson's generous gift.

Later, the grey cat led the five tiny creatures through empty alleyways and darkened streets. A cold wind blew, tearing at dustbin lids and scattering litter. They avoided late night revellers who made their way home from parties throughout the city. But it was time for them to return to Newgrange to rest and recoup their power. They stood on the outskirts of the city and said goodbye to Percy.

In the twitching of a whisker, the Shamrogues held hands and vanished in a swirl of dazzling colours. Percy made his way back to the house that he knew he would live in for many years to come.

CHAPTER THIRTEEN

A Chase

Some time later, after the Shamrogues had magically returned to their hidden quarters in Newgrange mound, Trendorn stirred from a deep sleep. The elderly badger was beginning to feel increasingly tired as the harsh winter bit deeper into the bleak land. But he couldn't spend all of his time resting in his comfortable straw-filled chamber dug into the stony clay of a tree-covered hillside.

Just as a rabbit's home is called a burrow, and a fox's is known as an earth, so Trendorn's was a marvellous place called a sett. It had five entrances and was filled with metre after metre of tunnels. These led off in different directions, each one having several rooms or chambers that for the most part were no longer used. Once the thriving home of generations of badgers, it was now empty except for the old male, Trendorn himself.

So, Trendorn was used to foraging for food under the cloak of darkness. Hunters were seldom about at night. But there were some nasty people who were willing to take the risk of badger baiting. This wicked pursuit was not a nice prospect for any animal that should be unfortunate to find themselves on the receiving end.

Trendorn's black and white striped face, with lively eyes and a shiny black nose at the end of a long snout, appeared at one of the entrances to the sett. His wedge-shaped silvery haired body followed the small head into the clearing in front of the sett. Trendorn raised his nose and sniffed the air to see that everything was as it should be.

A Chase

When he was satisfied, he ventured a few paces further and sat on the beaten mud. It was time to begin his nightly ritual.

First, the elderly badger shook the bristles out of his fur. He took some moments doing this, and then he enjoyed a good scratch. The close confines of the interior of the sett barely allowed him room to take pleasure in such a glorious pastime. Having finished grooming, he rose and checked the air again. Then he was off at an ambling trot on a well-worn path, one of many he had to choose from, to the opposite side of the hill. He limped along, feeling the annoying stiffness in one of his rear joints. Head low, he continued for a while with his larger hindquarters swaying from side to side. Occasionally he stopped to listen to his surroundings as he made a lot of noise himself and needed to pause.

Then he was off again. "Pad, pad, pad, pad… stop…listen…pad, pad, pad, pad, pad, pad…stop… listen…" And so on until he found something tasty to eat, or arrived at his destination.

During one of these many pauses, Trendorn heard something that strikes terror into the heart of any badger who is far away from his sett. His tiny white-tipped ears picked up the sound of a breaking twig in the stillness, and then something far worse – the voices of human beings, his most unfeeling and dangerous of enemies. He immediately froze and considered what action to take.

Although frightened, the badger held his ground and weighed up the situation. From previous experience he knew that it might be an accidental meeting. But this was highly unlikely since another unsettling noise carried on the wind – the anxious, almost inaudible yelps of small hunting dogs. So that was their game; they were carrying out a search of the coppice!

They were still some distance away but seemed to be heading in his direction at a steady pace. Using his acute hearing, he lowered his head close to the ground.

He could hear footfalls; one, two lightly…then one, two heavily. Rustle, scratch…scuff scuff…on and on. There were two men accompanied by two dogs, and they were drawing nearer.

As they did so, they began to pick up speed. This could mean only one thing. The sharp noses of the dogs had picked up Trendorn's scent and they were entering into the chase with alarming interest. It would be their job to seek him out. The hunters, who were most likely armed in some way, would use a well-tried method to catch him.

Trendorn broke into a loping trot and decided to make things a little more difficult for those who were on his trail. He began to barge his way through the densest undergrowth he could find in his path. The badger zigzagged and, at least on one occasion, criss-crossed his own scented track. Throughout, he remained level-headed and alert. It was of the greatest importance that panic should not take over. Just one mistake could cost him his life. The main thing was to cause confusion to his pursuers.

"This is sheer madness, Daly. We'd need to let the dogs off their leashes. They're dragging us around in circles and I'm being torn to shreds by all these brambles and thorny bushes. We can use the lamps to keep an eye on where they get to." The voice was gruff and agitated.

"I know what you…MEANNN!" There was the crashing sound of a low bush being crushed by the fall of something heavy. It was succeeded by a series of howls and yells that rent the night apart.

"I told you, Daly," the gruff one said. "Now you've gone and tripped. Serves you right!"

"Stop all the pontificatin', Brazel. Help me to my feet before this blasted dog pulls my arm out of its socket. We'll use the lamps as you say."

Because the men had come to an abrupt halt, Trendorn was forced to move very slowly, lest they should hear him. He found it much easier to creep along in a crouched position, his immense knowledge of the undergrowth and the area he was in serving him well. He headed for an old disused badger sett that had been turned into a warren of rabbit burrows. The furry creatures had dug smaller holes that led off the much larger tunnels. A plan was already forming in the wise badger's brain, but he still had some way to go. He heard the loud yapping of the dogs as they were allowed freedom from their leads. High treetops reflected light from the strong lamps that the two men had switched on in pursuit.

Trendorn had to move quickly. It was not very far now, but he was beginning to tire with the unexpected effort his body was having to make. All the time, the dogs dashed closer and closer.

Fear drove the hurrying badger onwards. Then something nipped and tried to hold onto his short tail. He skidded on sodden leaves and angrily turned, teeth bared, snarling, ready to fight to the death.

He was surprised by the sight of only one dog, but heard the other barking in the background as it steadily caught up on its companion. The Jack Russell who faced Trendorn found it very unsettling to have to tackle such a formidable opponent alone.

The badger suddenly charged and drove the dog back. Thinking it to be the wiser decision, the Jack Russell retreated to wait for the Bull Terrier. The men were a long way off, but the harsh cries of the dogs as they closed in on their quarry gave them their lead. The two men depended greatly on the dogs. They scanned the forest high and low with the powerful beams of their torches.

Trendorn seized the brief moment of opportunity to make his escape. He scurried as fast as his legs could carry him to the dilapidated sett that he had grown up in as a cub. Rabbits were untidy creatures by comparison and had let the diggings decay almost to ruins. Still, it was the safest place around. Having looked back only once, the elderly badger sped inside and bolted down a familiar tunnel. The two dogs were not yet in sight.

Some rabbits were alerted by Trendorn's stampeding charge past the mouths of their burrows and looked quickly out. But then they heard the barking of the dogs as they approached and knew that it would be much safer to mind their own business. They had their own lives to think about.

Once at the entrance, the dogs squabbled over who should go in first. The Jack Russell put up a feeble argument. He had already been close to the snarling badger and knew him to be a mighty foe who would react savagely to any attempts to drag him out. The disagreement was short-lived. The two men arrived with their blazing lamps and called the dogs to heel.

In the brightness, they studied the sett and its surroundings. Many stout sycamore trees cast weird shadows as the men moved about and checked the ground for recent tracks.

"Those blasted dogs have made a mess of everything. They've done so much jumping about that they've destroyed any tracks. The only other ones that I can see here belong to rabbits."

As Brazel spoke to Daly, he rubbed his sweating forehead with a grubby piece of rag. The other man knelt and studied the marks more inquisitively. His shifty eyes narrowed and he fingered the trodden surface. He sniffed a wad of mud he had plucked from the entrance.

"Seems like you could be right. Admittedly, this is an old sett. Those fool dogs must have picked up on some wandering rabbit."

Trendorn, who had made his way as far as he could without having to dig further, listened intently to every word that was being spoken. Luckily for him the dogs had been called off.

"I knew we shouldn't have bothered coming here," the gruff voice of Brazel moaned. "There haven't been any badgers on this land since my grandfather's time. I'm fed up agreeing to your stupid plans."

"I swear," Daly insisted. "I heard there was a badger seen about these woods. It could be only rumours though. But we've waited too long already. I've had enough."

"There's no use trying this sett, I suppose. Even the dogs are sick of rabbit stew. The dopey mutts should never have led us here. But I know a place where we will definitely have some luck tomorrow night." Brazel spat into an untidy heap of rotting leaves.

"Where?" Daly asked. "You should have said before."

"Well, there's a whole load of badgers living under protection right in the middle of Brockalaun Woods. It could be worth a try if you have the bottle. We could go there in the van after midnight tomorrow when all respectable cruelty-to-animals people are tucked up safely in their nice warm beds." Brazel chuckled and spat once more.

"I'm in," Daly said. "Maybe we should bring more dogs. These two won't be enough for a big job. Let's go."

Trendorn heard them leave. Then, later, he made for the dump.

CHAPTER FOURTEEN

The Dump

In the meantime, deep inside Newgrange, the Shamrogues were becoming increasingly bored. Having had a taste of life outside the enchanted mound, they were finding it difficult to stay underground.

But the five little creatures discovered that they needed time to recharge and top up their powers. Using their magic to zoom home from Dublin had drained them entirely.

Caffa, the old druid, had chosen their place of concealment very well. It was not only an ancient historical site, but also possessed mystical properties that revitalised the Shamrogues with the energy they needed. Rest was the best way to recover and it also gave them a chance to think about and discuss what they had already learned.

"I'm fed up," Glic said to the others in the darkness of the chamber. "I feel we've been in here for so long that I know every nook and cranny off by heart."

"I'm fed up as well," Gorum complained. "But I've thought about our situation very carefully and have come to the conclusion that we have no other choice."

There was silence for a while, then Sona said happily, "Let's play 'I Spy'! We always have a lot of fun with that game!"

"Phooey," Croga exhaled. She looked around the chamber with eyes that had seen it a thousand times. "I'm tired of such silliness. What's in here? There are only stone walls and a flagstone ceiling, and an earthen floor that's cold and damp. It's worse than Miss Crilly's basement. 'I spy'. my foot... There's no excitement in that game any more!"

Trom listened with growing concern. This unrest was not healthy for the good of the group. Still, he had to admit to himself that his own nerves were becoming a little frayed. Something would have to be done before they were all pulling their hair out by its roots.

"Enough complaining," the leader said without raising his voice. "We all know why we have to stay in here. But we could make it a bit more comfortable. And I have to admit that, having seen how people live nowadays, our surroundings are very sparse by comparison."

"We could do the place up to our own liking," Glic suggested. "We've seen lots of useful things lying about outside."

"Awww! Outside, outside," Gorum moaned. "That's all you can think about. There are more important things in life than outside."

"What?" Glic retorted. "Tell us what is more important, knowitall!"

"Why…there's…ehhhh." Gorum blinked and rubbed his chin in deep thought. "There's…ehhh… Well, there's a lot to be learned in historic monuments like this." He pointed all around him.

"Pah!" Glic was about to carry the debate further.

"Hold it," Trom ordered. "That's enough!" He looked intently at his four companions. "If this is an indication of how grown-up humans behave then we should have remained as stones. From now on we have to act in a more civilised manner."

Trom stopped talking and inhaled. He could see that his words had found their mark. The other Shamrogues appeared to be ashamed of their foolish squabbling.

Trom quickly came to a decision. "Perhaps we could take a moonlight ramble. It's the safest time for us to venture outside. Anyway, some fresh air wouldn't do us any harm. What do you all say?"

There was no need for the leader to ask twice. Eyes popped open in the dark chamber. The stirrings of restless feet and the rubbing of tiny hands together gave Trom his answer.

"Right," he said. "Even though we have not fully recovered our powers, we deserve a break."

"When?" Glic asked excitedly. All eyes were focused on Trom. "I think now would be as good a time as any," he answered.

There was a rush for the tunnel that led to the outside world.

"Civilised," Trom sternly reminded them. "Think civilised."

The four hurrying Shamrogues had some trouble trying to untangle themselves from the mouth of the exit. When they eventually managed to step back, they looked with crestfallen faces at Trom.

"Civilised," they chorused with one voice. Trom nodded and peered from beneath his bushy eyebrows.

They then left one at a time, Trom taking up the rear. Sona took the lead and began a happy chant. The others quickly joined in as the wonderful feeling of movement and adventure coursed through their little bodies.

"OGHAM, OGHAM, OGHAM," they continued until they stood on wet grass and stopped to take deep breaths. The night air made them shiver and they began stretching and flexing as they gazed around the open countryside.

Clouds raced across the sky, driven by a strong wind, heading for the distant sea. High above these, a full moon peeped between the dark fluffy formations and shed great patches of yellow light on to the earth below.

Gorum sniffed the air and made a funny face. "I smell food somewhere. The memory of Miss Crilly's scones has me thinking all kinds of things. Is it my imagination?"

"It comes from over there," Sona said, pointing.

Trom said, "From how far off?"

"It can do us no harm to find out," Glic said, eager to get going.

"Let's get through the fence and follow our noses," Trom said.

"Yay," Sona said, beaming. "At least this time we can relax!"

"Carefree, with no mission on our minds," Glic commented. "This is going to be great!"

Trom followed a little way behind. He was amused by the antics of the others as they came across bits and pieces of disused farm machinery.

Gorum looked closely at a broken plough that had only one remaining wheel and was rusted over so badly that it seemed like the bark of a gnarled tree had grown over it. When he concentrated on trying to make it move, the old implement merely groaned and remained stuck in the ground.

Croga, while climbing through a shallow ditch, found what turned out to be crisp bag. Of course, she hadn't got a clue what it was, and thought it might make a useful cover to keep the cold away. She promptly dragged it over her head and pulled the bag all the way down to her feet with a self-satisfied grin on her face. Only seconds passed before she was gasping for air.

The other Shamrogues were amused by her frantic struggles. Croga fell over and toppled into a steeper part of the ditch and landed in a deep puddle. Muffled screams escaped as the bag began to sink. There was a gurgling sound as bubbles broke on the surface of the muddy water.

Glic and Sona started to howl with giddy laughter. They thought that Croga must be having immense fun, but Trom and Gorum knew better and exchanged alarmed glances.

"What can we do?" Gorum cried.

Trom's heart began a giddy gallop. They would have to act swiftly if Croga was to be saved. Bubbles ceased to rise to the surface. "Magic," he said. "Make the water evaporate this instant."

A cloud of steam formed and then vanished just as quickly. Suddenly the ditch was empty of muddy water and the soggy bag lay there lifeless. Sona and Glic stopped laughing. The joke had gone too far.

"Don't stand there," Trom snapped. "Get Croga out!"

Gorum, Sona and Glic sloshed through the squelchy mud. They tugged at the wrapper and were horrified when it rose lightly in their hands. Mystery of mysteries, it was completely empty!

"Nothing here..." Gorum said and swallowed hard.

The others were lost for words.

Suddenly, there was a plopping sound from behind them. They wheeled around as a mud splattered stone rolled slowly to drier ground.

"Zop!" Two popping eyes emerged on the top. "Ssplunkk! ssplunkk!" Two grubby hands appeared and scraped away mud from what turned out to be a mouth. "Fladdop! Ffladdopp!" Two feet wriggled free.

A miniature mud monster stared at the other Shamrogues. The eyes blinked as the creature shook herself free of filthy wet slime.

"I certainly didn't enjoy that," Croga blurted. "But, being able to turn to stone at a moment's notice has its advantages. I'll never try anything so hair-raising again."

The others breathed a sigh of relief.

Trom wiggled one of his fingers at an overhanging branch and thousands of tiny droplets showered Croga. She trembled in the downpour, but was soon as yellow and clean as she had been earlier. Her red hair seemed brighter than ever.

"Can we continue?" Gorum pleaded. "The smell appears to be getting stronger. And it's doing funny things to my insides."

Croga shivered. "Brrrrrr," she uttered. "I hope there's somewhere warm nearby. I'll catch my death of cold."

"Come on and we'll find out," Glic said.

The Shamrogues trooped onwards. Soon they came to a spot that had once been a quarry. But the site was being slowly filled in with all types of useful things. It seemed like paradise to the five creatures as moonlight lit up the whole area. Moonbeams bounced off shiny objects.

"What is this place?" Sona asked and her eyes sparkled at what she saw. "It's lovely!"

"There's a million different remarkable smells now," Gorum said, sniffing. "It's hard to tell one from the other."

Trom made an unpleasant face. "What a horrid stink."

The Shamrogues began to rummage enthusiastically, each one finding something interesting which may come in handy in future.

"AAAAGGHHHH!" Sona shrieked. She pointed at a flat thing that rested against a rotting wooden plank and glared at her. It forced her to jump back in fright.

The others ran to her aid and were equally startled.

From somewhere inside the flat thing, five identical Shamrogues were staring at them. They dived back and hid behind whatever cover they could find. There were tense moments as they waited for the other creatures to step out. But for some reason, it never happened.

Croga, realising there was no immediate danger, stood out from behind a slug-eaten head of cabbage, and strode boldly forward.

"EEEEEK! There's still one of them left. And it's coming after me!" she shuddered and reeled backwards.

Trom caught her beneath the arms as she nearly fainted. He put her gently sitting on a torn piece of blue cloth.

"Things are always happening to me," she whined. "It's much safer back in the boring chamber. No ugly creatures there."

The leader marched a few paces and then moved slower. Harumping, he stepped in front of the flat object and studied what he saw. The other Shamrogues peeped and watched.

Trom put his hands to his face and twiddled his fingers. He rolled his eyes and stuck out his tongue. Then he hopped with difficulty on one foot. There were deep throaty chuckles that grew louder and louder as the leader had an uncontrollable fit of nervous laughter.

Sona and Glic were the first to join him. Gorum was next. He raised himself on tiptoe, and peered over bobbing heads. What greeted him was the sight of his companions' reflections.

"Croga," he called. "It's all only a marvellous trick."

But she refused to move. Two frights in a short space of time were more than enough for her.

The Shamrogues paraded and cavorted in front of the mirror until they got used to it. Looking at their own reflections for the first time was a funny experience. Sona could not be coaxed away from admiring herself, and constantly rubbed her pink skin and ran her slim fingers through her brown hair.

Trom found a used toothpick with one end broken off, and began to prod and poke around with it. He speared a green round soft ball and didn't recognise it.

Glic tapped on the side of a long cylinder that was large and round, and closed at one end. The can had a label on it with a picture of many more green balls.

He called Trom and showed him. The leader studied the letters, and, using magic, he turned the word into understandable language. "P-E-A-S," he read, and then said the word. "The round green things were peas."

Trom was delighted with his new found ability. But the elderly leader was becoming a little tired. He sat down on a page from a magazine with an advertisement for women's make-up.

Glic found a tube which he picked up with great difficulty and carried over to Croga who had recovered from her earlier shock. Unfortunately, she was in no mood for any further excitement.

Trom called to her. "It's called lipstick. According to the words printed here, if you spread it around your mouth, it's supposed to cheer you up."

Croga was baffled. The others gathered around and urged her to experiment with the strange substance called lipstick. After much cajoling, she reluctantly agreed. She stuck a finger into the tube and took some out. Gingerly, the yellow creature spread the smudgy mess around her thin slit of a mouth. The colour matched that of her hair.

"Go and look at your reflection," Sona advised.

"Go on," Glic encouraged.

She needed no more persuasion.

"OOOOOH! Is that really my own image? If it is, I'm pleased," Croga declared. "That other ugly creature has vanished." She blinked and smiled broadly at herself, the lipstick stretching the full width of her face. Having folded her arms, she tried every different angle to view her profile.

"Instant vanity and self-obsession," Gorum muttered to Trom. The leader smiled.

Unwittingly, Glic pressed the button on the top of an aerosol can. A thin sweet-smelling vapour hissed out and covered the rear of Croga from hair to heel. It turned out to be hair lacquer, and it nearly stiffened her rigid.

She moved with difficulty and climbed into an old cardboard box, refusing to come out until the others were ready to leave. But they still had some exploring to do.

Trom felt somewhat rested and resumed his probing. The broken toothpick was proving to be very handy. Glic found something similar and was thrilled with himself. It was a small ornate fork with two sharp prongs for jabbing cocktail sausages. He held the silver fork above his head and gave a blood curdling cry like a warrior of old. With wide sweeps, he waved it in the air.

"No one will dare mess with me now," he cried.

Gorum felt sorry for having sprayed Croga. He dusted off the piece of blue material that she had been sitting on during her fainting spell and passed it into the cardboard box to her. She carefully wrapped the blue strip around her body. What with lipstick and a blue garment, she could have been mistaken for something other than a Shamrogue. At least, that's what she thought.

Sona had come across a toy doll's brush and needed no telling as to what it was. Almost glued to the mirror, she tried several hairstyles, but, try as she might, her hair insisted on springing back into its usual shape.

"I need some of that hair hardener," she said.

Trom shook his head. "I'm afraid not, Sona. When you see what it has done to Croga, I think it's best not to meddle."

Gorum searched for an elusive smell. He delved through a mountain of tin containers of all sorts. Strange, stale odours escaped from some of them. Finally he found a dainty egg-cup with a thin line of a crack in its side. He claimed the prize as his very own.

"I'm bringing this back to the chamber with me," he insisted.

At the same moment, Glic discovered something which would serve as a ready-made mattress. He bounced on its surface. It had once been used as a bathroom sponge. He jumped so high that he felt as though he was flying and then he came down to land on his back. As he did so, something caught the corner of his eye. He lay still and gestured for the others to hide.

Trom hid behind a smelly milk carton and listened. Something large was shuffling through the mound of grubby items. There was the sound of heavy sniffing. With clinking and rattling and puffing and blowing, the noise came nearer.

The carton was abruptly pushed aside and Trom knocked into a gooey concoction of stale yogurt and mashed potato.

"What the...!" he yelled. He peered up into alert hungry eyes and saw a black and white striped face.

The other Shamrogues heard him call a familiar name.

"Trendorn, you mighty animal, you almost flattened me. We hadn't a clue who was rumbling through this place of treasures."

The badger gazed around and smiled. "Treasures?" he said. "My father, and his father before him called this a rubbish dump. I don't know where they got the name from, but that's what an area like this is known as. Humans throw the things they have no further use for in a place such as this. Then they cover it over with clay and pretend all this mess was never here at all. They love to fool themselves, poor creatures!"

The Shamrogues laughed at this. Then Gorum said, "But there are some very useful items to be found here. We are going to bring some of them back with us to the chamber."

"Most animals find things of use in this place. Magpies and jackdaws are attracted by shiny things and bring them to their nests. Others gather wool for its softness."

Trendorn sat down and took a long, heavy breath. Trom, who was engaged in wiping away the mess he had fallen in, noticed there was something wrong with the old badger. Not wanting to be too direct or nosey, he began polite conversation.

"Well, what have you been up to since we last met?"

The badger didn't have much to tell, but eventually came to speak about being chased by the humans and their dogs.

"As you know," he continued. "I'm getting on in years. No longer am I able to run as fast as I used to. The hunters almost caught me with the help of their vicious dogs. Luckily, I found an old badger sett to hide in until they decided to give up. Then I had to come here because I'm so hungry. With this cold weather, I've been forced to stay inside and haven't eaten for days!"

"What did you hear them say?" Trom asked.

Trendorn explained that he had never learned how humans speak. "But I did catch one single word which is the name of a place. It's in another valley a fair bit away, but many badgers are supposed to live there in safety."

"Where's that?" Gorum inquired. "They must have mentioned the name for a special reason."

The badger appeared to be in deep thought at the suggestion. "Brockalaun is the place. It's a woodland of great beauty. I suppose they are going to hunt there since they failed to catch anything tonight. The badgers will not be expecting a raid. And there is the smell of death from those men, so my relations must be in great danger."

Trom considered Trendorn's story. "We must warn them. Protect them, if we have to. Will you come?"

"I will lead you," the badger assured the Shamrogues. "In fact, you can travel on my back. We will need to start out early tomorrow evening. Now I must build up my strength by having some food."

"We'll collect what we intend to bring back to Newgrange. Already we have some things of interest chosen," Trom said.

Croga climbed from the cardboard box to help. She had heard everything and looked forward to another task. Boredom would be kept at bay, for another while at least.

Gorum watched Trendorn as the badger went about foraging for food. It was an interesting lesson, full of nudging things out of the way and nibbling at what was uncovered. The little blue creature imitated as best he could, but only ended up with a dirty face. "There must be something more to it," he thought. His nose was, by this time, totally confused by all the peculiar smells and stinks.

Trendorn found a juicy earthworm and quickly swallowed it whole. Gorum searched beneath a soggy newspaper and found a lesser earthworm.

He immediately put it to his mouth. It wriggled in a demented fashion. Gorum sucked and slurped and drew it into his puckered mouth. With a little noise like the sound of a pebble dropping into a pond, the tail-end of the worm vanished. Gorum jammed his mouth shut.

"How was it?" Trendorn asked as he licked his lips.

"Mmmmmmm....mmmmmmmm," Gorum muttered. His mouth worked as though it wanted to explode. He turned a paler shade of blue and scrunched up his face.

"Yaaauukkk!" he spat the still wriggling worm out. He rubbed at his mouth and wiped his tongue.

"Horrible. Food is horrible. How could children possibly eat it?"

Later, when the novelty of the dump had worn off, they discussed plans to meet Trendorn the following evening.

CHAPTER FIFTEEN

Brockalaun Sett

The old badger limped to the boundary fence and awaited the arrival of the Shamrogues at the ground-level opening. His limbs ached from the exertion of the chase during the night before. Now he stood at Newgrange and watched the mound with a feeling of expectancy and anticipation. Never before had he known the thrill of actually wanting to be of help to other creatures of his own kind. If it had ever been the case in the past, he had forgotten because of old age. Having left his own sett earlier than usual, he looked at the grey sky above as the last streaks of light descended to the west. There was a long uncertain night ahead. Anything could happen and he was bothered by a niggly uneasiness that he could not explain. He yawned a little nervously and shook the troubled thought from his mind.

Faintly, at first, then louder and louder, the sound of the marching chant reached Trendorn's ears. The Shamrogues were on their way. "OGHAM,

OGHAM, OGHAM," they intoned in a happy mood as they came up to the badger. He greeted them with a warm smile and stooped so that they could climb onto his bristly back. Without delay of any sort, they were immediately on their way. Excited conversation soon started.

"That was the best night's sleep I've ever had," Glic remarked as he was tossed and bumped up and down on Trendorn's broad back. "My new mattress is as soft and comfortable as a bundle of downy feathers." He held on tightly to a tuft of fur with one hand and carried the cocktail fork aloft in the other.

Trom, who rode up at the front, brandished the toothpick. Croga wore a thin strip of blue material on each wrist and a wider band about her head, the loose ends trailing in the wind.

Sona looked more radiant than ever. She had scooped up some of the lipstick substance into a piece of paper the previous night and had drawn two parallel red lines about her laughing mouth. The reflection sheet – she did not know the word "mirror" – had been of immense help with the make-up and she had spent a lot of time experimenting in front of it.

Gorum sat gloomily at the rear and was bounced up and down higher than any of the others. He was not enjoying the free ride.

"We should have used magic to get us to Brockalaun Woods," he complained.

Trom explained from the front. "I'm surprised at you, Gorum. You should know that had we done so, it would have exhausted some of our power, which has not had enough time to come up to full strength. We might need every grain of magic energy we possess. Trendorn has been gracious enough to bring us. Anyway, he knows the way and any short cuts that could save us valuable time."

"I'm sorry," Gorum muttered. "I'm worried we may be rushing into things. Something doesn't feel right about this mission. Those two men sound as though they're very dangerous, and they're bringing mad dogs with them. With our powers not fully up to scratch, we could be tackling more than we can cope with. The thought of that and all this bumpy movement has me in a jittery frame of mind."

Sona was totally optimistic. "We're only going to warn the badgers, silly. They can go and hide until the men have given up their search. Then everyone can get back to normal. So just enjoy the jaunt!"

But Gorum still felt a sense of foreboding.

Trendorn trotted over the crest of a heathery hill and stopped. The Shamrogues peered to the spot he pointed out to them with a nod of his snout.

"Brockalaun Wood is on the opposite side of this valley. The sett is half way up the slope, close to the centre, I believe. Some forestry roads run by it, and a wildlife ranger lives in a cottage down by the nearby stream."

"That could be useful information," Trom said as the badger continued down the hill to the trickling water. When they arrived, Trendorn quickly found a ford where they could cross to the opposite side. The Shamrogues dismounted as the old animal took a long drink of the cool liquid that was clear and fresh.

"We can make the rest of the way on foot," Trom said. "There's no need to cause alarm to the badgers who live here. You should go ahead Trendorn, and let them know of our approach. We'll stay out of sight until you call us."

He made his way up a well-scented trail to the enormous sett. When he was still some metres away he paused and listened. There was the scuffling sound of harmless rough-play. It was a noise he knew well but had not heard in ages. He felt his pulse quicken at the prospect of meeting others of his own kind, and let out a series of shrill yells to alert them of his presence. Everything immediately became silent. Soon there was the urgent sound of scampering paws. Trendorn walked slowly forward until he came to a beaten mud clearing in front of a dozen entrances to the large sett. There was not a single badger in sight but he knew that eager ears were listening.

He sat down and patiently waited. A strong deep voice called out to him. "Who are you and what is your business here?"

The old badger explained who he was and where he had travelled from, adding, "I have come to warn you of the threat that faces this sett tonight. Little friends are with me to help. They are known as Shamrogues and you have never seen anything like them. They are willing to do whatever they can to stop two violent men with dogs from destroying your home."

A badger, almost as old as Trendorn, walked cautiously from an entrance that had the appearance of being well used. He was large and powerful looking, his coat being a shade darker than the older badger's. But, size apart, he had an intelligent face with soft understanding eyes.

"My name is Natchanter. I am leader and protector of this community. How am I to know that what you tell me is the truth? We have lived here for many years in peace and have no cause to fear any human. They have kept this location for the continued use of us badgers. Why should they want to harm any of our kind after all this time?"

Trendorn looked earnestly at Natchanter. "These are evil men. They believe they will catch this community off guard. Then they'll slaughter many, and take others away for their wicked sport of baiting. The strong and young will have to fight many vicious dogs, who crave nothing else but the smell of blood. I bring you this bad news with a great sadness in my heart."

Natchanter looked over his muscular shoulder at the sett. His small ears twitched at the tiny feeble yelps that came to them. He slowly shook his head.

"Lupait, one of our fairest females, has given birth to three cubs this very night," Natchanter said. "We were celebrating before you arrived. The news you bring is indeed alarming. Neither she nor her cubs can possibly be moved. We'll have to confront this threat!"

"I understand," Trendorn almost whispered. "This will be a difficult night. May I call my friends to join us?"

Natchanter's mind was already concerned with the serious matter of defence. He summoned his own close-knit family that was made up of two more adult males and three females. Lupait remained with her baby cubs in a cosy chamber at the rear of the sett.

Trom led the Shamrogues into the clearing. The badgers' faces were full of surprise and amazement as they watched the arrival of the five small creatures. It was the different colours and their strange body shapes that caused most interest.

Natchanter approached Trendorn when they were all assembled and rubbed noses with the old badger in an ancient way of greeting amongst their kind. "Welcome to you and your companions. I hope that between us we can cope with this coming attack."

"Never fear," Trom assured the other leader. "We have a few tricks to fall back on." Natchanter was astounded. The creature could speak in badger language.

Preparations would have to be undertaken with the utmost speed. There were some things that could be done in the sett for protection.

Trom and the Shamrogues watched the badgers gather into a huddle, Trendorn included.

"We must undermine some of this ground in front of the sett," advised Natchanter. "The men's weight will act against them when they try to get to the entrances. As soon as they step on the crust of earth, they will fall through into the holes we have excavated underneath. At least that will slow them down."

"And I suggest we close off the tunnel to Lupait's chamber," Trendorn said wisely. "She and her cubs can remain safely inside. A snout hole in the roof will give her more than enough air."

Natchanter nodded at the old badger's wisdom. "Then we will wait in some of the safer chambers for the dogs to commence their attack."

"It appears we won't be needed at all," Gorum said lightheartedly. "These badgers seem to have everything under control."

Trom was also impressed. "Nevertheless, we will remain here in case our help is required," he said.

"I want to do a bit of digging with this," Glic announced, and waved the cocktail fork in the air before jabbing the prongs into the ground.

Trendorn padded over as the other badgers went about their various tasks. "They have some chambers inside that are situated in protected recesses beneath buried boulders. Male badgers will lie on these and drop on any intruder who tries to pass. You will be able to watch what goes on from the safety of one of these chambers. Now, I'm going to help the others."

CHAPTER SIXTEEN

Badger in the Bag

The Shamrogues watched the fevered activity as the badgers set about their various tasks with determination. They reconstructed the tunnels in no time at all, to make it a problem for the terriers that would be coming to invade the sett.

A tour was in order, and Trom led them through the maze of lofty clay passages.

"We should move to some place like this," Croga said.

"It all looks so complicated," Glic said, and thrust his fork into the clay beside him. The prongs disappeared as the wall collapsed and opened into another passage. The green creature fell through and was covered in a fine layer of powdery soil. "See what I mean? Complicated!"

Gorum and Sona began to help him up. Trom raised the toothpick to quieten their frivolous chattering. Croga ran to the nearest exit and peered outside.

"There are two searching beams of light that look like fiery eyes," she called back into the sett. "And there's the sound of one of those great monsters with wheels."

"That's them. The hunters have come in the dead of night to wreak havoc. Everybody to their positions," Natchanter shouted. The Shamrogues tucked themselves into a chamber that had once been a nursery. Trendorn climbed up over the opening into a tight alcove. They were as ready as ever they would be. Lupait would keep her cubs quietly content, until, hopefully, all the fuss was over.

The sound of the van died down with a splutter and was taken over by the impatient husky barking of dogs. Then there were voices that rasped out snappy commands.

"Heel!" one of them cried. "Heel, you cur, or I'll put my boot to your backside. Come on, Daly, that sett is nearby. Get the gear out of the van while I manage these four mangy mutts.... And don't forget the lamps."

Daly took two shovels and laid them on the ground. Then he grabbed a long-handled pincers known as a badger tongs. It was a cruel implement that gripped an animal by the fur and skin, and allowed the poacher or hunter to hold the helpless badger at a distance from them. Lastly he picked up a tightly woven sack and the lamps. He grappled to get them all into his arms and awkwardly followed Brazel, who had gone ahead.

At the edge of the clearing, they stopped to study the sett. Brazel, who wore a floppy cap that came down to his dark eyes and nearly covered the back of his thick neck, tethered the dogs with ropes to the branch of a tree. His old army jacket was ripped under the armpits and his baggy trousers were full of pockets, where he carried a penknife and bits of wire and material to make snares. Heavy thick-soled boots, that had not seen polish since the lazy fellow had found them in a dustbin, were tied with bits of string for laces. He looked around at Daly as the younger, unshaven man dropped what he carried to the ground.

Daly's head was covered with a grubby woollen bobble-hat. His long face wore a whining expression, and his eyes darted nervously about. A long grey coat reached almost to his feet. He tramped around in leaky black Wellington boots.

"Get the lamps focused on the entrances," Brazel said, scowling. "Then we'll send in the Jack Russell to sound out where those badgers are lurking. Have the shovels ready to start digging, and keep the tongs handy. I'm in humour for some sport." He chuckled and spat on the ground.

The dog rushed forward in the glaring lamplight and disappeared down the nearest sett entrance. It was also the one that led straight to the chamber where the Shamrogues had taken refuge. Trendorn snarled as the Jack Russell bounded towards them.

Outside, the other terriers yapped furiously and strained at their leashes.

The old badger was about to counterattack, but Trom emerged from his hiding place and stood in the path of the dog. The leader of the Shamrogues aimed his toothpick between the animal's eyes. A misty beam appeared as Trom concentrated. He mumbled a short rhyme in dog language.

> *Into our chamber, you will now creep.*
> *So don't be bold, just go to sleep!*

The dog wore a mystified expression as his body slowed down so that he appeared to be walking in slow motion. His eyelids drooped and his tongue lolled lazily out the side of his mouth. He grinned foolishly as he passed Trom and entered the chamber beside the other Shamrogues. They stepped aside as he curled himself into a comfortable place at the back and rested his chin on his front paws. With one heaving breath he fell fast asleep.

It was not very long before Brazel and Daly became impatient. They paced up and down, shovels in hand, ready to dig as soon as they got some response from the Jack Russell. But the dog was enjoying a merry dream about being a carefree puppy once again.

"Shut those damn animals up," Brazel snapped at Daly. "I'm going closer to get a better earful of what's happening below ground. Keep the lamps trained on those entrances."

Brazel stalked forward and tried to move lightly, but he was a very heavy man. No sooner had he got within a couple of metres of where the dog had entered the sett, than he let out a panicky gasp as the ground gave way under him. Falling lengthwise, he tumbled into one of the excavations that Natchanter had ordered to be made. Then the sides caved in on his struggling shape and nearly suffocated him. He dug his way out with his hands, losing his shovel and floppy cap in the effort. His head appeared above ground as he spluttered a mouthful of gritty mud from his mouth. Brazel crawled back to Daly.

"Send another blasted dog in," he snarled. "I'm going up to the top of the sett. They might think they're being smart by setting traps in front, but all we have to do is approach from another direction. Give me your shovel. I'll be more careful this time."

A lowly mongrel with a debatable pedigree was the next one to be let off her leash. Being a mother herself, she didn't like the job that the two poachers had brought her for. At first, she considered running away. Brazel frightened her, though, and she slowly sniffed her way to an entrance to the sett from which

a slight breeze blew. It could mean only one thing. She stooped and entered, hoping she would not come across a badger. And then a chance she had been waiting for presented itself. The tunnel, with several empty chambers right and left, led straight to the rear of the sett where there was an exit. She crept out. Silhouetted against the glaring light over the top of the mound, the black form of Brazel stabbed the soft earth with the shovel. But the man could not see beyond the blinding fringe of light. The mongrel took the opportunity and made her escape into the dense trees of the forest.

When there was no sign of the second dog, Brazel lost his temper and began to dig for all he was worth. "We'll put the remaining two dogs down into the sett as soon as I find a passage. And don't forget the badger tongs. I'll drag one of those animals out of it yet!"

Daly did as he was instructed, minding to evade the front part where Brazel had fallen in. He hauled the whimpering dogs behind him. They, too, were afraid of the older man. The lamps still blazed on the whole scene.

The Shamrogues listened to the commotion that now went on above their heads. Trendorn had jumped down from his perch above the slab and joined them. The clatter of the steel shovel as it hit grit and stones, the restless yapping of the dogs, the angry talk of the men as they worked themselves into a sweaty frenzy all sounded thunderously close in the confines of the muted chamber. The Shamrogues emerged into the passage.

Then suddenly something terrible happened! The pointed edge of the shovel broke through the roof of the tunnel and was quickly ripped back out again.

The Shamrogues were momentarily confused as to whether they should make a run for it or duck into another chamber. They waited.

Trom said something in a hurried whisper to Sona. He then told the others to pay attention to what was happening overhead. Clumps of soil fell in on them as slanting rays of light broke through.

"Prepare," Trom urged. "It appears we are going to have to be the first line of defence. The badgers are in other parts of the sett and we will have to tackle this problem ourselves. Good luck to you all!"

With a final crash, part of the roof tumbled into the passage. Two fearsome faces glowered into the illuminated opening. Before anybody could do a thing to prevent it, the dogs were flung bodily downwards. Confusion followed in a hectic scramble of flailing limbs as dagger sharp teeth slashed through turbulent air but connected with nothing solid.

"I'll draw these savages off," Trendorn roared. He tore at the dogs with bared fangs and then retreated back down the tunnel. "It's me they are after. Shamrogues! Deal with the two humans."

The dogs, keeping a distance all the time, pursued the brave old badger and snapped at his heels.

In the glare of the powerful lamps, Brazel and Daly could not see properly into the hole but they knew that the dogs had made contact with a badger.

"The tongs," Brazel said. "Get the jagged jaws of them into this opening, quick. I can barely make it out, but there's movement down there."

Daly knelt down and began to probe with the cruel implement. Keeping the handles apart, he was ready to snap them shut on anything that moved.

The Shamrogues rubbed their eyes as they stumbled blindly around. The falling particles of loose clay from the ceiling of the tunnel had created a storm of gritty dust in the confined passageway. A thick fog of powdery material floated about and almost choked the tiny creatures, and they coughed and sneezed in the suffocating haze.

With one hasty sweep, the tongs brushed off Gorum as he blundered about. As his eyes were smarting and closed, he caught the side of the pincers, thinking it to be one of his companions. Daly felt the sudden resistance and lifted the implement a little and then jabbed it back down into the hole. He slapped the handles closed and began to withdraw the tongs as something squirmed on the end.

"AAOOWWW!" Gorum screamed. "I've been grabbed by the hair. HELLLP! OUCHHH!"

Glic was the first to clear his eyes and he saw Gorum's blue feet ascend past his face. He was frightened by the loud screams and quickly realised that something was wrong. He made a short running leap and swung onto one of his friend's feet.

Thinking that something else was tackling him from below, Gorum struggled even harder and tried to kick Glic away. Suddenly the weight that tugged on his foot got heavier and he was nearly pulled into two halves. He grabbed above him and held onto the top of his aching head.

Croga had been lucky enough to catch sight of her two companions as they were drawn upwards. In the clearing haze, she caught onto Glic's feet, and was lifted towards the surface. She would try to save them.

"I've got hold of a fine big one," Daly enthused as the handle of the tongs juggled in his hands. "Open the sack and hold it near the hole. I can't see a thing with those blasted lights. Hurry before it wriggles free!"

Below, Trom was greatly alarmed by the terrified cries, but was still unable to clean the grit from his eyes. Sona took hold of his arm.

"Those bullies have Glic, Gorum and Croga, and are bundling them into a stinking sack," she said, trembling with panic. "Ohh, what can we do?"

Daly dropped the tongs and whipped the sack from Brazel who had knelt beside him. "I'll get this back to the van! Then we'll load the rest of the things and get out of here."

"Attend to what I told you earlier," Trom uttered to Sona, "immediately, or all is lost." She scampered away as fast as her tiny feet could carry her.

Brazel glared into the hole. "I can hear another badger. We might as well have it as well. I'm going to have a go with the tongs. Get yourself back here pronto."

Trom blinked several times and his eyes began to see the horrible tongs approaching him in the dark tunnel. He then began to make out the ugly leering face of the big poacher. The leader of the Shamrogues was determined to put a stop to the two men. He worked magic so that the tongs reversed themselves and took on a life of their own. Trom directed them with the aid of the toothpick. The handles turned into the pincer end. The jaws became controlled by an invisible force and suddenly latched onto Brazel's left ear. The poacher screeched and howled as the implement began to tug him into the hole. His head, with loose strands of greasy hair hanging in all directions, filled the opening like a stopper.

"Hel...Help me," Brazel pleaded as his eyes grew accustomed to the near darkness and he saw Trom for the first time. It never occurred to him that he was talking to a creature no higher than his ankle.

"Harump!" the leader of the Shamrogues scolded. "You're a despicable person, and so you shall learn what it's like to be hunted through these tunnels." Trom pointed the toothpick.

As big as you are, it's time to see!
By magic shrink as small as me!

The poacher's eyes bulged in their sockets as the spell worked on him. The tongs released his ear and he swiftly became one hundredth of his former size. With a frightened yelp, and then a thud, he fell headlong into the tunnel.

Trom walked towards him with the toothpick at arm's length. Above ground, through the huge vent, they heard Daly calling the dogs in an urgent voice. In the passageway, Brazel backed away from the leader of the Shamrogues. Abruptly, he felt something nudge him in the back. Turning, he saw the menacing long teeth of Natchanter. The badger closed in on him. Uncontrollable fear gripped him and he ran down a side tunnel on legs of jelly.

Daly had nearly reached the van when he felt a sharp stabbing pain in his shoulder accompanied by a clatter of hard thumps. The badger in the bag was beginning to bite and struggle. After two more piercing nips, he threw the sack to the ground.

Luckily he had tied it tightly with a piece of string. It wriggled and rolled about. He would leave the wretched animal there for now. In the distance, he could hear the barking of dogs and the high-pitched yells of a badger as they engaged in a battle for survival.

Further down the valley, Sona reached the Wildlife Ranger's house which was in complete darkness. Now, where would the Ranger be asleep? She walked around the lodge, eyeing each curtained window. One in particular caught her attention. She thought hard and willed herself to be on the windowsill. In a moment, Sona found herself precariously perched beside a small pane of glass. There was no sound from inside, but lots of other noise filled the upper part of the valley.

Sona rapped on the window and waited... nothing! Could her instincts be wrong? She knocked again, this time much harder. Seconds ticked by...and still nothing.

"Wake up," she willed. "Wake up and help us."

Barely had she finished, than she heard a muttering voice in the bedroom. It approached the window. The curtain was wearily pulled aside, and the dishevelled face of a woman peered out. Then her gaze settled on Sona, who had reverted to stone.

"What is it, dear?" a man's voice called sleepily.

"Somebody's throwing rocks at the window. Oh, and there's loads of blazing light on the trees up in the wood. Maybe it's a forest fire." The curtain was dropped back into place. Sona willed herself to the ground.

In a moment, the curtains were torn back again and the window thrown open. A man with a young thin face leaned out and almost fainted with what he saw and heard.

"It's not a fire, Mabel," he hoarsely said. "It's an invasion by poachers. I can hear the dogs going mad. Quick...while I throw on some clothes...call the police, ring the army, muster the civil defence, get them all! There's nasty work afoot in the valley!"

Sona heard all she wanted to hear and made her way back with speed to the sett.

In the sack, the three captured Shamrogues waited impatiently. "We could be out of here with little bother," Glic said.

"But we might be able to serve a better purpose here," Gorum argued. "At least, as long as we remain, those ruffians will think they have a badger."

Croga rearranged the blue band around her forehead. "Already they seem to be getting ready to leave. They sound like they're happy enough with what they've caught."

"This fork has come in handy," Glic said. "I can enjoy some more fun with its sharp spikes. They make very authentic badger nips. What a night this has turned out to be!"

Gorum caught him by the arm. "Quiet, there are footsteps returning. We need to tumble about a bit to make them think they have a lively badger."

Of course, Gorum was not to know that Daly was alone. Brazel was still being stalked through the labyrinth of tunnels in the sett, without being quite caught. Natchanter and his friends would let him know what it was like to be hunted and cornered.

"Brazel has done a bunk," Daly said. "The coward has left me here to do all the tidying up. Well…not me." He picked up the sack. "I have what I came for. If he wants to go rambling in the night, then that's his business. I'm off."

Daly called the dogs for the last time and threw the sack into the van while he waited. He put two dirty fingers into his mouth and let out a long low whistle. Only one single terrier came lamely out of a thicket of brushwood, blood on his short coat.

"Get in the van, you stupid mutt. You've got what you deserved. Still, you haven't deserted like the rest of them. Now, time to get out of here."

Just as the poacher sat into the van, Sona arrived on the scene. The man started the engine, but it barely got going before it died down and stopped. "Blasted dampness in these woods," she heard him whine. Then she heard him roar in pain. The sack on the seat beside him had delivered another stinging nip. Glic was being busy. The poacher shoved the grubby bag to the floor of the van as he turned the key again. The engine sputtered.

Sona spied thick black smoke escaping from the exhaust.

"I must put a stop to that pollution," she said to herself. A wad of heavy mud, stuffed down the black pipe, did the trick.

The engine coughed and wheezed and then gave up for good. Without being able to exhale the foul smoke through the exhaust, the van would never start. Daly made an effort to open the only door in the cab of the van that worked. But it had jammed solid and, try as he might, it refused to let him out. He became frantic.

Then the noise of blaring sirens filled the valley. Very soon, a string of cars with flashing blue lights on their roofs were seen to approach along the country road.

Brazel, who was about to run to one of the exits, with badgers in threatening pursuit, started to grow back to his own size. He was halfway out when he became wedged in the opening and could move no further. Half in, half out, he screamed for help. Full-sized humans should not try to use badger tunnels.

Uniformed policemen arrived and surrounded the area. The Wildlife Ranger was with them and he ran to the van and opened the door with no problem. Daly was taken out, and the sack along with him.

"It's only a lousy badger," the poacher protested. "And hardly worth the trouble. That rat Brazel must have spilled the beans on me. I knew he was setting me up!"

With that, Brazel was wrenched from the entrance and brought to join the other man. He was delirious from his experiences, and mumbled and dribbled. "An old lad with a toothpick attacked me. The badgers chased me through the sett and tried to eat me. I was small…so small."

"Small minded," a police sergeant said. "I've been after you for quite a while, Brazel, and I've never heard such drivel to try and get sympathy. We caught you down a tunnel, kicking at a badger no doubt. This time you're really nicked. Come on, there's a spare cell at the station just waiting for vermin like you."

The two men were led away. Opening the sack, the Ranger saw three stones and a cocktail fork. One of the stones had blue ribbons tied around it. He tipped out the stones. "I'll keep this fork as a souvenir in memory of tonight," he said. "Those poachers are a right pair of looneys. They even thought that a few stones were a real live badger. Heh! Now, home to bed for me!"

Soon, when the cars had sped away, the valley became silent again. The Shamrogues felt it was safe once more to gather in the clearing with the badgers. The police had removed all the poachers' equipment.

"That turned out to be a hectic adventure," Trom said.

"One we could very well have done without," Natchanter added. "Now I must check on Lupait

and her cubs. Then we can get things back to normal. There are repairs to be done."

The badgers got to work, busily and in earnest.

"Where's Trendorn?" Sona asked happily. "He'll be very proud of how we handled things after he drew those nasty dogs off."

"I hope he's okay," Gorum said.

"We'll wait and see," Trom said. "He's probably waiting in hiding until he's sure the coast is clear. When he returns, we can make our way back home with him. Let's rest until he arrives."

CHAPTER SEVENTEEN

Back to Newgrange

The pale winter dawn of a new day spread across the morning sky. Erc the raven soared high on an uplifting wind and scanned the earth below in the endless search for food.

A slight movement beside a brook caught the attention of his trained eye. He spiralled slowly down, allowing the wind's current to help him glide on broad, black outstretched wings. Round and round, down and down he went, never taking his eyes from the object below. He was used to behaving in such a manner on his searches. When he was low enough, he smoothly flew down to land on the soft grass. He strutted the rest of the way to the bank of the small stream. The sweet smell of blood and death was everywhere. He often found food where odours of that type filled the air, but it was always sensible to be extra careful at times like this.

Erc looked down at the gravel bank of the trickling stream. The back of a gravely wounded animal, its snout almost immersed in the water, met his gaze. The bulk of its body heaved as it took a painful gasp of breath. The raven walked to the badger, his wings ready for instant flight. He was deeply shocked when he discovered it to be Trendorn, an acquaintance of many years.

The old badger turned to look at Erc. Trendorn's eyes flickered with lingering life. He attempted a smile. His left forepaw was badly gashed, and the water around it ran pink. Another great wound had been inflicted to his neck. The raven knew that the situation was hopeless. He had seen many things happen in his long lifetime, but this was one of the saddest. He knew that Trendorn must have travelled so far from the safety of his own valley for some very special purpose.

Bird and badger could not talk directly to one another in their separate languages, but animals possess an understanding amongst themselves, a sort of mental knowledge that lets them communicate their thoughts to one another. Trendorn made his intentions known to Erc in this way.

"My dear friend, Raven," the badger thought. "I would like you to do me a favour, if you will. Just one request from an animal who has never asked anything of anyone."

"All you have to do is make it," Erc answered in his mind. The raven stepped closer to the badger's head. "I will do whatever is in my power."

"I want you to make contact with my friends, the Shamrogues," Trendorn thought and gasped. He pushed himself back from the water's edge with difficulty and continued. "They are the little creatures that crawled from the gap between the boulders on the morning of the great gathering at the enchanted mound. You and I watched from the hillside, do you remember?"

Erc thought for a moment. In his mind's eye, he could see the scene as the sun crept over the horizon and he could hear the thunderous noise before the peculiar happening. It had been a moment he would never forget. "I do remember," he thought.

"Well, they await my return in Brockalaun Wood at the huge badger sett. Both they and I came here to warn my cousins of impending danger from two poachers with four dogs. I myself tackled two of the thoughtless animals during the attack. I drew them away from the sett and we ended up doing battle here. It was a very fierce fight and I received these wounds. Then one of the dogs broke off and ran back into the woods. The other fought bravely on. He neither took nor gave any quarter, and we fought for a long time. I feel sorry for him, really. He was never taught anything else. He had a cruel life himself and only obeyed his master's commands."

"He too ran away?" Erc questioned.

"No," Trendorn thought sadly and swallowed hard. Although he had already taken water until he could take no more, his mouth felt dry and parched. "The terrier lies dead about ten paces from me in that clump of bushes at the top of the bank. It's terrible that his life had to be wasted."

The raven knew that it was pointless to look. And what could he say or think that would make any difference now?

"But how will these Shamrogues respond to me? I have never been one to approach those whom I do not know."

"They understand the language of all animals. The Shamrogues have such powers. Please tell them I am here."

Erc looked at Trendorn. "This is the last time we will meet, mighty friend. I have not the heart to return. Your spirit will soar higher than I have ever flown. Don't be afraid, for it is the way of things… Goodbye."

The raven took to the sky, not daring to look back. It was better this way, and he had a favour to perform. He swooped to the sett in the woods where he saw the Shamrogues waiting on the stout trunk of a fallen tree in the morning sunlight. Erc landed beside them and immediately began to tell them about Trendorn and where the badger lay. It was not a time for introductions or lengthy conversation. He only said what he had to and sadly took to the sky yet again.

Trom called the leader of the badgers and told him what had been said by the raven. Although it was daylight, Natchanter called his followers and they decided to go to Trendorn. The Shamrogues and badgers marched to their loyal friend. When they came near, Natchanter told Trom and the others to go ahead of himself and his companions.

The old badger raised his head slightly as the Shamrogues came near to him. He blinked his weary eyes in recognition that they were there. As they gathered round, he began to speak in a low whisper.

"My faithful friends, my time has finally come. I'm a gonner and I've run my race. No longer will I see the new moon rise or savour the earthy smell of the chamber in my cosy sett. But it has all been well worth it. I see that all my cousins are safe and healthy. That is indeed good. And the five of you…I want to thank you for your help."

The Shamrogues were lost for words. Croga stepped forward and, without saying anything, stroked the fine badger's forehead. Then she went to his injured forepaw and, removing the blue ribbon of material from her head, tenderly wrapped it around the wound. Then, not knowing why, she kissed Trendorn on the snout. Having done this, she walked away and stood alone.

It was a signal to the others. Silently, they did the same thing and one by one went to join Croga. When it came to Trom's turn, the badger opened his eyes as wide as he could. He spoke so quietly that the tiny leader could hardly hear the words he uttered.

"Don't be sad, Trom. I've had a good and long life. I want to thank you all. I can never say it enough."

"You don't have to say it at all," Trom said. "Is there anything we can do?"

"I'm afraid not. Natchanter and the other badgers will look after things from here on. Matters like this are dealt with in a special way. When the time comes, I will be buried in a remote chamber of the sett. It is the custom. My last wish will be for the terrier who fought to the very end to be laid beside me, and then both of us walled in. That way, neither of us shall pass on alone. But your tasks have just begun. Already, you have helped others who were in need of assistance. I hope you all have great success in the future. The world is a most mysterious place which mankind has chosen to abuse. I know you will do your best to change things. Now, I am very tired and will say farewell. Please remember me…"

Trom walked away. He waved to Natchanter and the other badgers. They would carry out his wishes.

The Shamrogues followed the course of the water towards the bigger stream. They did not speak for a long time. Finally, Trom felt there had been enough silence.

"What happened back there is the way of the world. Trendorn sacrificed himself so that three little badger cubs might survive. He was old and knew exactly what he was doing. Our thoughts are with him, but life must go on."

"That's right," Glic added. "Why, we have millions of things yet to do. I may even find another pronged fork."

Gorum shook his head. "You're heartless. Always thinking about something you can get into mischief with."

"Well," Croga said and folded her arms across her chest, two strips of blue material still around her wrists. "We did help out where the chemical plant was concerned. And Miss Crilly is happily living in her own house because we went to Dublin. I'm sure we will meet some pitfalls in the future. Brockalaun Woods was just the first."

"That's exactly it," Trom declared. "And we did help to save the sett. There will be many more places that need our attention."

"The dump," Glic enthused. "People will need to be educated about not throwing so many useful things away."

"You're obsessed with useful things," Gorum moaned. "Why don't you try to think of something else. Think of all the pollution from those metal monsters that zoom along the roads. Even the noise they make is…"

Trom raised a hand and pointed to Sona who sat apart from the rest. She stared at the crystal clear water of the stream and was silent. The Shamrogues watched her face. Something strange was happening.

Two glistening tears ran slowly down her cheeks and sparkled in the sunlight like precious jewels. Trom went to her and put an arm around her. In her own little way, she was perhaps the wisest one of all. But the Shamrogues understood. The tears were not those of sadness, but tears of hope for the future. Trom gently wiped them away.

"Right, Shamrogues. Back to Newgrange…!"